THE HERE
AND NOW

ANN BRASHARES

THE HERE AND NOW

h

Hodder
Children's
Books

A division of Hachette Children's Books

First published in the USA in 2014 by Delacorte Press, an imprint of
Random House Children's Books, a division of Random House LLC,
a Penguin Random House Company, New York.
Produced by Alloy Entertainment

First published in Great Britain in 2015
by Hodder Children's Books

A Catalogue record for this book is available from the British Library.

ISBN: 978 1 444 92192 2

Printed and bound in Great Britain by Clays Ltd, St Ives plc

The paper and board used in this paperback by Hodder Children's Books
are natural recyclable products made from wood grown in sustainable
forests. The manufacturing processes conform to the environmental
regulations of the country of origin.

Hodder Children's Books
A division of Hachette Children's Books
338 Euston Road, London NW1 3BH
An Hachette UK company

www.hachette.co.uk

For dear Isaiah, captain of family time travel.

And for the smart, patient, generous editorial team without whom this book would not be: Josh Bank, Beverly Horowitz, Wendy Loggia, Leslie Morgenstein, Sara Shandler, Katie Schwartz and Jennifer Rudolph Walsh. Thank you.

The past is a foreign country: they do things differently there.

— *L. P. Hartley*, The Go-Between

If time travel were possible, we'd be inundated with tourists from the future.

— *Stephen Hawking*

◆ PROLOGUE

April 23, 2010
Haverstraw Creek

His dad had to work, so Ethan had gone fishing alone. Usually he just followed his dad through the woods to the deep bends of the creek, slapping at the prickers around his ankles. This time he was confounded by how little he knew his way even though he'd been here again and again. After today, though, he'd know.

When he finally came upon the river, it was a different part than he'd seen before, but same water, he thought. Same fish. He put his pack down, baited his hook and made a good cast. It was different when he was alone and his cast was for catching a fish instead of showing his father he knew how.

He listened to the water and tended his line and considered the stillness of the air. Except for that one part over there. Downstream it seemed like the air was moving. He squinted at it, then opened his eyes wide and closed them again, wondering if he'd wash out the strange impression that the air was rippling over the stream. But it still looked like that, more like that, air moving and scattering in a way that he could see.

He edged downstream, pulling his line along. As he walked he could see far past the bend to a footbridge. And at that distance the air and the leaves were still. But here the air moved faster and seemed to quiver like the water. As he moved slowly toward it the air took on a strange texture. He squinted again and saw in amazement how the sunshine seemed to refract into colors around him. He walked a few more steps and felt the air moving faster over his skin, almost like liquid but softer. He wanted to focus on pieces of the splintering light, but it was all moving too fast.

He lost hold of his fishing rod as the liquid of the air seemed to blur and blend with the liquid of the stream, pulling him inside the brew. He lost his hold on what was above and what was below, what was sky and what was earth, what there was to breathe, or even where his body began and ended. The odd thing was, he didn't feel the urgent need to find out. It was like a lucid dream in that he occupied no part of the world he'd seen before, but he knew he would wake up from it.

He had no idea how time passed, whether there was a big cascade of it or almost none at all. But at some point the spinning churn of river and air coughed him onto firm ground, and slowly the elements went back to their ordinary places. He closed his eyes for a time, and when he opened them again, the river was mostly in its banks, and the air went back to being invisible and the sunshine had reassembled itself. He sat up and gradually reoriented himself to basics like up and down. The storm produced a scoured, sparkling look through the trees, and it also produced a girl.

She was almost certainly part of his dream in that she was not quite made of regular-girl substance. The outlines of her weren't quite distinct. She was the kind of girl he would dream up because she was approximately his age, her skin was bare except for the dark wet streamers of hair around her body, and she was supernaturally beautiful, like a mermaid or an elvish princess. Because he imagined her he felt it was okay to stare boldly at her.

But as he did it dawned on him that her arms were clutched around her body like she was cold and also embarrassed. Her legs were muddy up to her knees. He could hear her rough breathing. The longer he stared, the more details she accumulated, the more distinct her lines became, until he began to suspect she was real and that he shouldn't keep looking at her like that.

He stood up, trying to keep his eyes mostly down. A couple more glances convinced him that, though the air around her remained oddly charged, she wasn't a nymph of his invention, but a shivering skinny girl with muddy feet and a weird bruise spreading from the inside of her arm.

'Are you okay? Do you need help?' he asked. It was hard coming back from the dream. She'd been swimming maybe, and had gotten pulled downstream by the storm. It was awfully cold to be swimming.

She didn't say anything. He tried to keep his gaze fixed on her face. Her eyes were big and her mouth was pressed shut. He heard the drip, drip, drips from the leaves around them. The sound of her trying to catch her breath. She shook her head.

'You sure?'

She shook it again. She looked like she was afraid to move.

She was real, but she was faintly different from anyone else, and not only because she wore no clothes. She was still beautiful.

He unzipped his damp New York Giants sweatshirt

and held it out, taking a few steps toward her. 'Do you want it?'

She shook her head, but she hazarded a look at it and then at him.

He took another couple of steps. 'Seriously. You can keep it if you want.'

He held it close to her, and after thinking a bit longer she shot out her arm and took it. He now saw that the blotch on her knobby arm wasn't a bruise at all, but a scrawl of black writing. There were numbers, five of them written by hand with a marker or something.

He looked away as she put on the sweatshirt and zipped it all the way up to her chin. She took steps backward, away from him. In his mind a dark feeling was coalescing that she had been though something difficult.

'I have a phone. Do you want to use it?'

She opened her mouth, but there was a space before any words came out. 'No.' Breath, breath. 'Thanks.'

'Do you need help?' he asked her. 'Are you lost?'

She looked around anxiously. She opened her mouth again but again hesitated to say anything. 'Is there a bridge?' she finally mustered.

He pointed downstream. 'If you walk that way, you'll

see it right after the bend,' he told her. 'Do you want me to show you?'

'No.'

'You sure?'

'I'm sure.' She looked sure. She stole one more glance at him, as though willing him to stay put, and took off toward the bridge.

He wanted to go with her, but he didn't. He watched her stumble off through the trees in his blue Giants sweatshirt, looking overwhelmed by the tangled branches and the knotty roots and the mud and the bushes grabbing at her.

Once she looked back at him over her shoulder. 'It's okay,' he heard her say faintly before she disappeared.

He stayed on the bank of the creek for hours before he went home. He looked for his fishing rod but didn't really expect to find it. He waited to see if the girl might come back, but he didn't really expect her to, and she didn't.

Through dinner and deep into the night he thought about what he'd seen. Finally he got out of bed and, picturing her skinny, shivering arm, copied from memory the numbers: 51714. Because he knew they had to be important in some way.

For the next two and a half years Ethan thought of that day so often his memory began to warp. So much that he began to wonder if he'd imagined the whole thing after all. Until the first day of his sophomore year, when the very girl, now clothed, walked into his precalculus class and sat down one seat behind him.

May 18, 2010
Dear Julius,

The earth sweats in the morning. Really. You can go outside here almost anytime, just like Poppy said. I like to lie down on the grass in the backyard and wait for the sun to come up. Even if there's sunshine for days, still the back of my shirt is damp, as though rain is wept from the ground.

Mr. Robert and Ms. Cynthia and a few others are in charge of most of the kids. They are trying to teach us how to fit in and always making us be EXTRA careful. Remember hearing about TV? Well, we watch it all the time to learn the right way to talk. One show is called *Friends*. People in the background are laughing the whole time and you don't even know why. The one I like is called *Family Guy*, but Mr. Robert said I'm not going to learn anything from that.

I'm worried because I haven't seen Poppy yet. Ms. Cynthia said he decided not to come at all, but I don't believe that. He wanted to come more than anyone.

Love,
Prenna

◆ ONE

April 23, 2014

We all know the rules. We think about them every day. How could we not know them? We learned them by heart before we came here, and they've been drilled into our heads by constant use ever since.

But still we sit, nearly a thousand of us, on plastic benches in a former Pentecostal church (desanctified in the 1990s, I don't know why) listening to our twelve inviolate rules recited over a crackling PA system by nervous community members in their best clothes.

Because it's what we do. We do it every year to commemorate the extraordinary trip we all took together four years ago: our escape from fear and sickness and hunger, our miraculous arrival in this land of milk and honey. It's a trip that almost certainly had never happened before and, based on the state of the world when we left it, will never happen again. So April 23 is kind of like our Thanksgiving, but without the turkey and pumpkin pie. It is also, coincidentally, the day Shakespeare was born. And died.

We do it because it's easy to forget amid all the sweetness and fatness of this place that we don't belong here, that we pose a danger to it. That's why the rules are critical and the consequences of forgetting them are grave. It's like any strict religious or political system. When your practices are hard to follow, you'd better keep reminding your flock of them.

I put my feet flat on the floor as the projector hums to action at the back of the hall, cutting a beam through the dark air and slowly illuminating the first face on the wide screen that hangs behind the old altar. It takes a moment for the shadows and shapes to become a person, to become someone I know or don't know. It's hard to watch this, but they always do it: as we recite the rules they show the faces of the people we lost since the last time we met here. It's like the 'in memoriam' tribute you see on the Academy Awards or the Grammys, but also . . . it's not. This year there are seven of them. There's no explanation or commentary. They just scroll through these faces again and again. But most of us have a sense of the story behind each face. We understand, without saying so, the overrepresentation of the fragile, the wayward and the incompliant members of our community up there on that screen.

My mother glances at me as Dr. Strauss stands up from the dais at the front to recite the first rule, the one about allegiance.

The rules are never displayed, never even written down on a piece of paper. That's not how we do things. We've gone back to an oral tradition.

I try to listen. I always do, but the words have been stirred around so many times they've lost their particular order and shape in my ears. They've melted and dissolved into a chaotic mix of impressions and anxieties.

Dr. Strauss is one of the leaders. There are nine of them and twelve counselors. The leaders make the policy and the counselors hand it down to us and translate it into our daily lives. We are each assigned to a counselor. Mine is Mr. Robert. He's sitting up there too.

A girl near the back in a green dress stands to recite the second rule, about the sequence of time. Heads politely turn.

It's an honor to get to recite one. Like landing a part

in the Christmas pageant. I was chosen once, three years ago. My mom dressed me in her gold ballet flats and her most expensive silk scarf. She mashed rouge into my cheeks. I got to say the sixth one, about never submitting to medical attention outside the community.

After the girl speaks, we all turn back to the front, obediently awaiting rule number three.

The black-and-white face of Mrs. Branch now takes its turn up on the screen. She was an acquaintance of my mother's, and I know she died of breast cancer that barely got treated. The photo doesn't exactly hark back to happier times. It looks like it was taken on the day she got her diagnosis. I look away. Briefly I catch the eyes of my friend Katherine a few rows behind.

I find it's hard to figure out from watching the leaders fanned out on the dais which one of them is really in charge. No one will tell you, but I think I know. I think this because of something that happened to me when I was thirteen, not long before my turn at reciting the sixth rule.

It was around nine months after we'd gotten here. I was still disoriented, still way too skinny, still watching TV to learn how to talk and act. I hadn't started going to school yet. I was having chronic breathing problems. My mom said it was really incredibly fortunate that somebody with asthma got to make the trip at all. She said something about my 'enhanced IQ' making up for it, but barely. We tried to pretend it wasn't as bad as it was.

And then in February I caught a bad cold and it turned into pneumonia. My mother knew this almost certainly because she is an MD and keeps a stethoscope in her bathroom drawer. A couple of other members of our community's medical team came over. I was pretty whacked by that point. I was using an inhaler and they were pumping me full of antibiotics and steroids and God knows what else. There was an oxygen monitor clipped to my finger, and I know it was dipping too low. I struggled. My lungs couldn't take in enough air. It's a horrible feeling, in case you've never had it.

By the second night it had gotten dire. I was completely out for some stretches, but I saw the look on my mother's face. She was shouting. She wanted to take me to a hospital. She said a simple ventilator for one night was all it would take to save my life. I guess we didn't have one in our community clinic then; we were still pretty new here. But putting me in a regular hospital wasn't something any of them would even consider because of the danger we pose to them, to regular people who were born here, who have different

13

immunities than we do. And because what if, in taking my medical history or getting too close a look at my blood under a microscope, a doctor or a nurse started asking questions?

'There's no need for her to die!' I heard my mother crying from the next room. She was begging them, promising she would watch over everything, she wouldn't let anyone else care for me. No blood tests, no diagnostics. She would figure out a way to do it, to keep everything secret and safe.

Sometime later Mrs. Crew arrived. I could feel the mood shift in the house, even deep in my oxygen-poor brain. The screaming and cajoling stopped and there was just this lulling voice from the next room. For a few moments I was strangely alert, strangely cogent, listening as she calmly talked my mother down. *After all we have sacrificed, Molly. After all we have been through . . .'* My mother left the room and I heard my counselor, Mr. Robert, talking to Mrs. Crew instead. I felt like I was listening to them from a perch on the ceiling, like I was already dead, as she coolly explained to him the procedure for dealing with my body, the issuance of a death certificate and the proper strategy for handling what remained of my identity in the state and federal databases. They had created our identities here; they could take them away. Finally she offered him some injection or pill or something like that. 'The angel of death,' she called it in a low voice, to make my passing more comfortable. She assured him she would stay until it was over.

But it wasn't over. Sometime in the early morning my lungs started to open up a little. And by the end of the day a little more. And six weeks after that I was reciting the sixth rule in this very hall.

Mr. Botts, two rows behind me, stands up to recite the third rule, about not using our knowledge to change anything. I remember him from our early tutoring sessions. Mrs. Connor, with the thinning hair and weird orange tunic, takes up the fourth, which is kind of an extension of the third. I forget how I know her.

A guy named Mitch, who's a star because he goes to Yale, recites the fifth one, the secrecy rule. That may be the rule we think of most often. The leaders are obsessed with the minutiae of it, with us fitting in and never letting anything slip that might give us away. But at times I seriously wonder, if one of us did let something slip, could anybody ever guess where we are from? And if they did, could they possibly believe it?

The sixth and seventh rules, the ones about medical stuff, are recited by two people I don't really know and who, like me, probably just barely survived those rules.

I zone out on rules eight through eleven because a purple bead pops off my shoe and I scan the floor for it without appearing to. I'd frankly rather look anywhere than at the big screen up front, because for the finale they've left up the photo of Aaron Green, and I suspect that's no coincidence. It's a heartbreaking picture of a confused and well-meaning fourteen-year-old who tripped over his lies so clumsily they stopped him from going to school in the middle of last year. His teacher went to his house to check on him, and two days later he drowned in the Housatonic River on a rafting trip with his dad and his uncle. There was no ambulance, no emergency room. Mr. Green quietly followed the protocol; he called the special number he was supposed to call.

I snap to attention for the twelfth rule. It is Mrs. Crew, the angel of death herself, who stands up to deliver it. She is about five feet tall and her hair looks like a cremini mushroom, but she still scares me. I swear she recites that rule staring directly at me.

◆

1.   WE MUST UPHOLD ABSOLUTE ALLEGIANCE TO THE COMMUNITY, TO ITS SURVIVAL AND ITS SAFETY, AND ACCEPT THE GUIDANCE OF OUR LEADERS AND COUNSELORS WITHOUT QUESTION OR DISCUSSION.

2.   WE MUST RESPECT TIME'S INTEGRITY AND HER NATURAL SEQUENCE.

3.   WE MUST NEVER EMPLOY THE EXPERIENCE GAINED IN POSTREMO TO KNOWINGLY INTERVENE IN THAT NATURAL SEQUENCE.

4.   WE MUST NEVER CHALLENGE THAT SEQUENCE TO AVOID MISFORTUNE OR DEATH.

5.   WE MUST UPHOLD ABSOLUTE DISCRETION ABOUT POSTREMO, THE IMMIGRATION, AND THE COMMUNITY AT ALL TIMES AND IN ALL PLACES.

6.   WE ARE FORBIDDEN TO SEEK MEDICAL ATTENTION OR SUBMIT TO MEDICAL CARE OF ANY KIND OUTSIDE THE COMMUNITY.

7.   WE MUST USE ONLY THE SERVICES PROVIDED BY OUR MEDICAL TEAM IN ALL CIRCUM-STANCES AND EMPLOY THE EMERGENCY PROTOCOL IF REQUIRED.

8. WE MUST AVOID INCLUSION IN THE HISTOR-ICAL ARCHIVAL RECORD, WHETHER IN PRINT, PHOTOGRAPHY, OR VIDEO.

9. WE MUST AVOID PLACES OF WORSHIP.

10. WE MUST MAKE STRENUOUS EFFORTS TO FIT INTO SOCIETY AND NOT BRING ATTENTION TO OURSELVES OR OUR COMMUNITY IN ANY MANNER.

11. WE MUST AVOID CONTACT WITH ANY INDIVIDUAL KNOWN TO US FROM POSTREMO WHO DID NOT TAKE PART IN THE IMMIGRATION.

12. WE MUST NEVER, UNDER ANY CIRCUM-STANCES, DEVELOP A PHYSICALLY OR EMOTIONALLY INTIMATE RELATIONSHIP WITH ANY PERSON OUTSIDE THE COMMUNITY.

TWO

A bunch of us get takeout from a Chipotle around the corner from the former Pentecostal church and walk with it to Central Park. The ceremony has fallen on a Wednesday this year, so we've taken a vacation day. We eat it on the Great Lawn and kill a couple of hours between the end of the ceremony and the beginning of the semiannual 'teen social'. Because our spirits are so light after the Rules Ceremony, why not have a party?

It seems crazy, but that's what we do. The night of the ceremony everybody in our community between the ages of fifteen and eighteen gets together and tries to fall in love with each other over dumb music and soggy chicken fingers. Good luck with that.

Because if we're going to love at all, or even like or

lust, we have to do it with each other. See rule twelve. And it's not just for our own safety, as the counselors are quick to point out. It's for the health and safety of the people outside our community too. It's not something you can even joke about. Not that we joke about so many things.

At the park it's me, Katherine, Jeffrey Boland, Juliet Kerr, Dexter Harvey and a few others who go to school in Rockland County. Jeffrey falls asleep in the sunshine, Dexter puts on his headphones, and Katherine and I go for a walk around the reservoir.

'So hard to see Aaron's face up there on the screen,' I say slowly, glancing at the side of Katherine's face as we walk. I see the color blooming in her nearly transparent skin.

Aaron lived around the corner from her. He had a little dog, a pug mix or something, named Paradox, that used to run to Katherine's house every chance it got. Katherine worried about Aaron. It was harder for him than for most of the rest of us. Maybe I worried too. Katherine gave Aaron her old Mongoose BMX bike, and you always saw him riding around on it.

I know how sensitive Katherine is, and I know she'll hide everything she can, but I want to say something. I want to say at least one true thing.

'He wasn't much of a swimmer. He never was,' I add. It's a morbid point for me to make. I realize that, but Katherine looks relieved because it's my way of telling her that I'm not trying to be too honest here. I'm not trying to challenge anybody. I'm accepting the story of Aaron's demise, as we all must, even though we know it is total bullshit.

She smiles a tiny bit. I can see the tears welling in her eyes. I see her look up at the cherry blossoms spread like an awning over the bridle path. I can see how much she doesn't want to cry.

I reach for her hand. I hold it for a moment and let it go. She is the only person I can do that with.

'They renamed his dog,' she says, so faintly I can barely hear her.

'What?'

'Aaron's dad renamed his dog Abe. He doesn't come to it.'

We all meet up again on the Great Lawn and head twenty blocks uptown, where we've got the big upstairs party room of Big Sister's Diner rented out. We usually have our gatherings in New York City because we all live within a thirty-mile radius of it and there's a lot of good transportation, but even more because it's so giant and chaotic it easily swallows everyone without a burp. We prefer not to be noticed.

Tonight on the second floor of Big Sister's there are streamers hanging and big foil pans of food laid out buffet-style and café tables set up around the room. Right at the front I see a few chaperones I recognize from other socials.

'Prenna? Right?' A woman about my mother's age with silver-and-black hair comes over as I'm taking off my jacket.

'Yes . . . Mrs . . .' I feel like I should know her name.

'Sylvia Teller. From, uh . . . We live in Dobbs Ferry,' she says. She looks uncomfortable. My mind is leaping around nervously, and then I realize it's just the usual reason. She was a friend of my father's. They went to college or graduate school together. She is racking her brains for a contemporary connection between us, because those are the only kinds we can mention, and she can't think of one.

I know I resemble my father, who was striking-looking and who knew practically everybody. I can see that's the first thing that comes into people's heads when they look at me. I am tall like him and have his straight dark hair and wide, Asian cheekbones. I look nothing like my mother, who is small and blond, except for the silvery eyes. Nobody ever connects me with her at these events but only, uncomfortably, with a person who can't be mentioned.

I don't want to feel sad. I go to the bathroom to wash my face and put on some lip gloss. I nearly slam into Cora Carter coming out of the bathroom and we both take a step back.

'Hey, Prenna.' She smiles.

'Cora. How's it going?'

We don't kiss on the cheek or embrace or anything. The people in our community hardly ever touch each other.

'Good.' She studies my outfit. 'You look great. I love your belt.'

I look down at it. 'Thanks. You look great too.'

'Did you see Morgan Lowry's bow tie?' She looks delighted about it.

'No. I just got here.' Morgan Lowry's bow tie is what passes for outrageous with us. 'I'll keep an eye out.'

'Okay. Well, see you in there.'

'Okay,' I say.

I realize I stay one second too long on her eyes, and it makes her uncomfortable.

I remember Cora from before. Everyone in our community came from roughly the same geographical area, and many of us knew each other in Postremo. We all have in common that we survived the plague, but none of us got through it unscarred. I remember the day Cora's mother died. I remember her half-starved, half-crazy eyes when her aunt brought her and her brother to our house until the body could be looked after. I remember a few months later when her brother died too. I don't want to remember these things right now, but I do. I have memories like this about at least a dozen of the kids here, and somewhere in them they have memories like this about me. Since we came here, the deepest conversation Cora and I have had is about my belt.

'See you.' She waves awkwardly and disappears.

I try to steel myself for a night of these kinds of conversations. Because these are the kinds of conversations taking place all over this room. No one talks about what really binds us together. The gap between what we say and what we feel is so big and dark that sometimes I think I'll fall into it and just keep falling.

At least, I think we feel it. I feel it. Does anybody else feel it? I don't know and I won't find out. We follow our scripts like actors in a very large, very long production. And even with no audience, none of us gives a hint that it isn't real.

Sometimes I only hear what we don't say. I only think

the things I shouldn't think and I remember what I should forget. I hear the ghosts in this room, all the people we lost in our old life who are crying out to be remembered. But we never do remember them. The whispers of things we feel and don't say – I hear them too.

Jeffrey puts a bunch of the little tables together, and a crowd of kids assembles, talking and flirting. He pulls a chair out for me and I sit down. I look at the people sitting around this circle. They are my friends. I care about them. This is my life. They are talking about their belts and their shoes and the car they want to get and the show they saw, and I can't hear them because the ghosts are too loud.

Around nine o'clock the chaperones help clear the tables to the sides of the room for dancing.

Jeffrey gestures to me, so we dance to a sugary pop song. Other kids dance too. I see Katherine dancing with Avery Stone, who is a letch.

If you pay attention, you see how awkward it is, how cautious and fearful we are of touching each other in the most casual ways. We can't help it. We spent our tender years surrounded by plague. I see the regular kids at our high school always grabbing at each other and hugging people left and right. Not us. We have no path to walk between physical isolation and hooking up. There's just the one and then the other, and I guess on account of the one, the other tends to be pretty jarring and impersonal.

Adrian Pond asks me to dance. He holds me around the waist. He is tall and good-looking, and I don't have any memories of him from our old life to haunt me. The song gets slower and he gets closer. His breath is warm in my ear.

I want to feel something. I really do. But it's only the absence I feel, just the wishing and wanting where there is nothing. I just feel lonely.

I lean my cheek on Adrian's shoulder. The lights over the buffet table blur and I close my eyes. I do something I should never, never do. I let myself think about someone else – a person I should never think about at a moment like this.

For a few seconds I give in. I let myself imagine it is his cheek I feel on my hair. I imagine his hands on my waist. I imagine him holding me like somebody who really knows how to hold a person. I imagine lifting my head and seeing his eyes, which really know how to look at a person, and he is studying me in the perceptive way he does, wanting stories from me I never tell him and seeming to understand me anyway.

It's wrong, I know, but I play out this dance with him, exquisite and slow. I play it out in my head, because that is the only place it will ever happen.

 **THREE**

'Hey, Ghouly. What's with you?'

I keep my eyes away. I work on the loose joint of my glasses. I can feel the blood heating my cheeks. If I look at him, I'm scared he'll see everything.

He nudges my foot with his. I pretend to be studying my notes very carefully.

Mr. Fasanelli turns from the board, where he's been chalking his way through a long calculus problem.

I glance at Ethan's fingers, his knee. Not his face. I should never have let myself think about him the way I did.

He's looking for something in his notebook. As soon as Mr. Fasanelli turns back to the board, he passes the notebook to me.

It's the hangman game we started last week. It's

already got its head and limbs.

J? I write without looking up. I pass it back.

Ethan gives the hangman a second chin.

K?

'Pren, you can't just go through the alphabet in order,' he whispers at me. He draws moobs on the hangman.

He succeeds in catching my eye. I let him hold it too long, and there passes all that I was avoiding: *You okay? What's the matter? Why won't you look at me today?*

Flustered, I grab the notebook. *Are there ANY letters in this word?* I write.

'Prenna, why don't you take the next one?'

I swing my head up. Mr. Fasanelli is staring at me. At the fat hangman. At me.

I look at the problem on the board. I rise and trudge toward it.

I can feel Ethan's eyes on my back. And from the deeper seats, I feel Jeffrey's eyes. Luckily, the bell rings to end the period before I have to do all billion steps of it.

Ethan has the nerve to be smiling at me on our way out of class.

I look down at the notebook. The hangman sprouted ear fuzz while I was suffering at the chalkboard.

'It was "wormhole".'

I look at him.

He points to the notebook. 'The word. With letters.'

'Oh. Right.'

'You should start with vowels, my friend.'

'Thanks.'

We hit the doors to the stairwell. Jeffrey is there too.

'Can I talk to Prenna a minute?' Jeffrey says, overtaking us before we pass into the chaos of the cafeteria.

Ethan glances at me. 'That's up to Prenna, isn't it?'

'Alone, I mean.'

Jeffrey steers me toward the windows. 'You should be careful,' he says.

'I am careful.' I watch Ethan instantly get swallowed up in his pack of soccer team friends. I miss his attention when it's gone. It is maybe the most astonishing thing I have. When I have it.

'More careful.'

'I am more careful.'

'About Ethan.'

I follow him out the doors to the walkway. Cherry blossom branches are waving along the walk, bits of flowers falling like pink rain. 'We are friends.' I realize I don't want to say Ethan's name aloud.

'Does he know that?'

'Yes, I think he knows that we are friends.' It's easy to play stupid with Jeffrey because he never really looks me in the eye.

Jeffrey takes off his glasses and wipes the lenses with his shirt. 'Does he know it's not more than that?'

'It never comes up. It won't come up.'

'You say that and I believe you. I'm just saying he might not see it the way you do.'

I walk faster. 'I can handle it,' I say. 'We are allowed to have friends, you know. We're supposed to have friends. We're supposed to fit in.'

'We're not supposed to have friends who look at us like that.'

I stop. I look at the flower bits on the sidewalk, under our feet, floating in puddles of yesterday's rain. I'm gripping my books so hard my hands are sweating. He doesn't know what he's talking about.

I can see Jeffrey feels bad. 'Pren, I just don't want you to . . .'

'I know,' I say.

'I don't want them to . . .'

'I know.'

He glances around to make sure we are alone. 'You know if any of these people find out the truth about us – no matter how nice and trustworthy they might seem –

they will destroy you and destroy all of us.'

How many times have I heard those words? 'I know,' I say grimly.

'Be careful?'

'I'm careful.'

Early that evening I hear the front door open and close. My mother is home, probably with dinner.

I finish my physics problem set and head downstairs.

Chicken, biscuits and coleslaw sit in bags on the kitchen counter. I get out two plates and two sets of silverware.

'Just take whatever you want,' my mom calls from the front hall, where she is going through the mail. 'I've got to finish confirming appointments for tomorrow. I'll heat some up and have it later.'

I leave the plates and silverware on the kitchen table. I'm hungry, but I'll wait.

Most teenage girls probably try to avoid having meals with their moms, but I'm the opposite. I'm always trying to corral mine into something that looks like a family dinner. The fact that my mom avoids it probably just makes me do it more. I guess a person rebels where she can.

My father was the one who was so big on setting the

table. He said family dinner was the backbone of civilization, and in our old life we sat down together night after night, five of us, then four of us, then three of us, even as the world was falling apart around us. That backbone didn't hold up too well.

I had two younger brothers who died within a few months of each other in the third dengue fever epidemic – the one that become known as the blood plague – the year before we came here. It is one of those facts, as true and cold as any other. It seems to me like a failure of language that that experience fits into a regular sentence made up of ordinary words. It fits into *one word*. 'Experience.' Just a regular old crowd of letters that doesn't care about you or your brothers. I picture using that as my next hangman word.

It is almost impossible to think of that 'experience' happening in the same life, in the same world we live in now.

My father, whom we called Poppy, survived the plague. I thought he was making the trip here with us, but he disappeared on the night before we left.

'He chose not to come,' my mother said, like it was just a case of cold feet or a more pressing obligation. But I know it wasn't that. I may never know the truth, but I know it wasn't that. I don't bring it up with my mother anymore. I can't bear the look on her face. He broke her heart too.

I go through the kitchen door to the deck beyond it. I lean on the railing and watch the sun go down. I search the sky for a crust of the moon.

I love this time of day. I love this time of year and the way our backyard comes to life with the wide white flowers of the dogwood trees and the clusters of daffodils that I myself planted. I can smell the verbena wafting from the bushes along the garage.

I've been here for four years, and I still can't get over how beautiful it is. At first it was all too jarring and strange for me to enjoy it — the sounds, the colors, the smells, the shocking sight of squirrels and birds and chipmunks, the fact of being allowed to be outside in the first place. But now I enjoy it every single day.

I am amazed by the lushness, the generosity of it, all the things you can eat and plant and pick, the places you can swim. People here act like the great things have already been lost, but they are wrong. They have so much still to lose.

I hear the sickening whine of a mosquito and I freeze. I listen for it with hyper-tuned ears, waiting for it to land, which it does, pure quivering evil on the wooden rail beside me. I fight back the impulse I learned as a very

34

small kid: never let a mosquito get close enough for you to slap. Now I take a nasty pleasure in smashing them when I can.

Back where I come from, mosquitoes represented our most primitive fear, the central fear all the other fears orbited around. We zipped our nets and sprayed our toxic sprays and said our prayers and huddled in our dark, decaying houses because mosquitoes carried death. It's hard to unlearn it, even now. They don't bring disease to this place, but for us they still bring memories and awful dreams.

Not yet. They don't bring death here yet. I stare at the nasty speck in wonder and revulsion. We're not afraid of the kinds of things people here worry about, like robberies and murders. Even the hurricanes and floods here are quaint compared to what is coming. This place seems almost laughably safe to us. The mosquito is the thing to worry about when the world gets wetter and hotter. Because when that happens, the mosquito's territory is everywhere and its season is always.

It's a wisp of nothing, its life barely bigger than a day. It has no will, no feelings, no memories, and for sure no sense of humor. I stare at it in sick fascination, waiting for it to make its next landing on my arm or cheek or ankle.

Maybe it does have a will. How else can you explain the number of its victims? Millions of people with big lives and heads packed with memories and all the stuff they knew – the accumulation of thousands of years of human history.

It is unfair. People versus mosquito. Who should win? We built rockets and cathedrals. We wrote poems and symphonies. We found a passage through time. And yet. We also wreck the planet for our own habitation and the mosquito will win. Unless we succeed in changing course, it will win.

Maybe it does have a sick sense of humor. I smash it under my palm. It will win, but not yet.

I see my mother through the kitchen window. I go back in and wash my hands. I see she's managed to thwart my table setting by getting a sole plate and hunching over the kitchen counter to eat.

'How was your day?' I ask.

'Good. Yours?' She's eating quickly and she doesn't look up.

'Okay.'

'Listen, I got another call from Mr. Robert this morning.' She's focusing on her coleslaw. 'According to him, you followed a stranger for four blocks yesterday and asked her about her rain boots.'

'Oh, right.' I should be contrite, but remembering it, I'm kind of excited. 'She had my old boots! You know, the bright blue rubber ones hand-painted with ladybugs and parrots and geckos? Do you remember them? I loved those!'

She's picking at her chicken. 'Prenna, the point is, that is red-flag behavior, and you know it.'

It's not the first time this kind of thing has happened to me. There are so many clothes now. But by the 2070s there was almost nothing new being made, and by the 2080s we were all wearing recycled stuff, a lot of it recycled from now. By the late 2090s, by the time we left to come here, most of it was in tatters. I've seen sweaters and scarves and jackets just like ones we wore. I once saw a man in a plaid vest across the street, and I followed him around for an hour thinking he could be my dad. That was red-flag behavior too.

'They aren't like my boots. That's what was so amazing. They *are* my boots. They are unmistakably one of a kind. I've always wondered who painted them. That's why I couldn't help asking. It was this twelve-year-old girl. She didn't look so great – I don't think she'd brushed her hair since Christmas. And she wasn't very nice either, come to think of it. But she was the artist! Pretty incredible. I guess your artist is never exactly who you want her to be.'

My mother looks up at me exactly once to indicate she is not enjoying my story. Katherine liked it better when I told her.

'Mr. Robert also mentioned he'd like you to do two extra counseling sessions this week and take the Saturday shift helping out at the office.'

'Seriously?'

'Prenna.'

'It was totally harmless.' I think a change of subject is in order. 'So, how's Marcus doing?' I ask, taking my plate to the table.

'He's, well . . . he's alive.' She starts putting the food away. I know she won't say more, and really, she can't say more. I can only imagine how hard it must be to go to her job at the community clinic every day and watch a boy with kidney failure not receive dialysis.

My mom got her medical training at the end of a golden age of technology, so it's got to be frustrating not to have so many basic things here. The leaders mostly won't take on big equipment that requires special training or certification. But these are not my mother's decisions to make, as she sometimes tells me.

She used to be a respected doctor and researcher, according to my dad, in charge of her own lab. It's hard to picture that now. Here she mostly does paperwork and schedules appointments. She came here wanting to prevent the plagues, and I'm sure that's what she cares about most, but I can see how the rules make it complicated. I don't think she's in charge of anything now.

I know this must be depressing for her, but not because she tells me so. She never argues, never complains. She rarely says much of anything at all, except to scold or caution me. She is an exemplary community member in that way. She eats and she works and she cleans up the house and she eats again and she reads, maybe, and she goes to sleep. Under her mosquito netting – that is her only quirk, her only concession to the past.

She's been through terrible things. Sometimes I think she's lost the idea of love. For her I think it's another luxury. It just makes it harder when you lose people.

No, that's not true. She loves me. I can see it in her face sometimes. It mostly takes the form of fear, when I say something or do something I shouldn't.

I set out two bowls and two spoons and a pint of ice cream. I sit down at the kitchen table, hoping she'll notice. I feel like at least one of us should hold on to what little we have left of our family.

She finishes washing her one dish and fork and turns to go. 'Good night, sweetheart.'

Unfortunately, I am alone in feeling that.

July 2, 2010

Dear Julius,

I'm trying to write and talk the way they talk here, but it's not easy. Thanks for letting me practice on you. It's just like Poppy said. All th-th-th-th-ths. People thalking through their theeth. Mom – I am supposed to call her Mom here, pronounced MAH-AHM – she gives me these worried looks when I mess up, but she can't really say the 'th' sound. She makes this wobbly rubber band shape with her lips.

She gets so uncomfortable when I talk about you or Poppy or anything from before, even by accident. I think the leaders and our counselors can hear everything we say. Not just in our house, but everywhere. I think that's why she's so nervous all the time. I'm not exactly sure how they do it, but I'm pretty sure they do.

I'm starting to think maybe Poppy really didn't come here.

Love,
Prenna

◆ FOUR

'Did you finish problem set C yet?'

Ethan rarely announces himself when he calls me. No *Hey* or *Hi* or *How's it going?* It's like in his mind we are engaged in a perpetual conversation that happens to be quiet a lot of the time.

I take a breath. I dread it's him and I'm glad it's him and I'm especially glad he can't see my face. I sit at my desk in my bedroom shuffling through my physics papers. 'Yeah.'

'Tricky, didn't you think? Those last two?'

'Um . . .' I find the paper. They hadn't been. Should they have been? 'Sort of. Not too bad.'

'Of course not, Henny. They were only tricky for the normal people.'

I recoil a little but say nothing. I know I find school

easier than most people. I am self-conscious about it. I'm not sure why I am this way — if it's because of my father's energetic homeschooling or if it's just a quirk of my brain. Sometimes I wonder if it's the reason they let me come here. To a different person I would say something like 'I already got to this section in a summer school class,' but I had vowed the first week I met Ethan never to tell him any inessential lies. He pays too much attention and has a strange gift for catching me in them.

'Can you show me how you did them?'

'Seriously? Have you tried turning off the TV?'

Ethan laughs and I am inordinately pleased with myself. Nobody ever teased me before I met Ethan, and when he first did, the language was as foreign to me as Swahili and at least as beautiful.

Ethan is very good at physics. He reads about string theory and quantum gravity in his spare time. He spent the last two summers interning at some kind of lab in Teaneck, New Jersey, that does research in theoretical physics. He does his homework while watching old seasons of *Breaking Bad*. He doesn't need my help, and he barely needs to do the problems at all. He's going to Columbia Engineering in the fall.

He once told me he calls me for the homework because I am the prettiest girl in AP Physics, which got my heart racing shamefully but doesn't mean a lot considering there are five of us in AP Physics and I am the only girl.

'Want to meet me at the library?'

I can hear in his voice he's just checking on me, seeing if I'm okay. I was acting weird this morning. I hear other voices in the background. Probably his friend Matt and some of the other guys from the sports blog he edits.

'No,' I say. What if I were honest? *I can't meet your eye because I am ashamed of the romantic fantasy I spun out between you and me the night of the Rules Ceremony.*

I pretty much never meet him anywhere outside of school or tell him anything he wants to know. I don't even make up excuses, because of the problem of lying to him. He is undeterred by this. It doesn't seem to discourage him that he calls me often and I hardly ever call him, or that he has about fifty dumb nicknames for me (Penny, Henny, Hennypenny, Ghouly, Doofus, James the First . . .) and I can barely bring myself to call him Ethan.

'I have a free period before lunch tomorrow,' I offer. I will pull myself together by then.

'I have Spanish. I'll skip it.'

'I thought you had a test.' I hate the scold in my voice.

I get scolded so often, sometimes I forget there's another way to talk.

'So I'll get there a little late.'

Ethan was the first person who talked to me the day I started ninth grade. It was the strangest thing. He was sitting in front of me in math class, and he turned around and looked at me like he knew me, like we were old friends with serious business between us, like he expected me to know him too. Two years later I am still trying to figure out that look.

It wasn't the kind of look I was accustomed to getting. I was this confused, weirdly dressed fourteen-year-old spouting canned lines from nineties sitcoms, whose classmates stayed as far away as possible. Except for Ethan. It was almost like he had something important to say, like he'd been waiting for me to show up.

I remember the thought that hung in my head toward the end of that school year, when I finally got up the courage to look at Ethan and not just my shoes: *Nothing bad has ever happened to you. You think the world is like this.*

He is a year older and the opposite of me in every way: invited to everything, liked by almost everybody. But he isn't your typical popular kid. His hero is Stephen Hawking. He has hair the color of Cheerios, which he cuts himself. He wears these oddball wool army pants even though they get shorter on him every month.

I've tried not to make too much of it. Ethan is genuinely nice to everyone, especially the underdogs. Since last summer, one of his favorite people is the homeless man who lives in the park and hangs out on a blanket in front of the A&P. Ethan calls him Ben Kenobi, and spends hours talking with him about quantum physics and whatnot.

Our last names are James and Jarves, and the school is very big on alphabetical order, so from the beginning Ethan steered me through a lot of picture days and field days and all-school assemblies.

I see myself kind of like the homeless guy in Ethan's eyes: a bit of a sad case, but an interesting one. More of a project than a friend. He knows something's a little off about me. Or suspects it. I can see by the way he looks at me, and I guess there is kind of a subtle alliance that goes with it.

I don't lie to Ethan, but I don't tell him the truth either. I can't. To share anything with him, even if I could, would put him in an impossible place. Already he is the drip, drip of water that carves a canyon right through the middle of me.

◆

The next Monday afternoon I sit in physics class gazing out the window at the bluest sky. I tune my ears to the traffic on Bay Street, and suddenly I'm deafened by the closer, louder clanging of the fire alarms in the hallway.

We take our time standing up and trooping to the door. Nobody looks particularly concerned. We join rivulets from other classrooms to form a stream down the hallway and then a raging river going out the side door.

'It's not a drill, it's a bomb threat,' I overhear someone saying upriver. The message makes its way back.

'Stupid seniors,' a girl to my left mutters.

It's a tradition, an unimaginative prank, for a senior to call in a bomb threat twice a year: once in the fall, once in the spring, usually on a warm and sunny day. It's as predictable as changing your clocks for daylight savings, but the administration has to take it seriously every time.

Faculty members are posted along the line, but we don't need their instructions to know what to do. I wish we could hang around on the football field and soak in the sunshine until the threat is cleared, but it isn't to be.

That's what used to happen, apparently. A few hours outside and then you got to go home. But finally the administration wised up and realized that the dismal Village Community Center is only two blocks away, and since I'd gotten to high school they'd started sending us there to make sure that the bomb threat posed as little fun as possible.

There is something humiliating about walking in a fat line down the sidewalk and across the street to the community center. It feels like nursery school.

We collect in the lobby to be shunted out to various rooms – alphabetically, of course. As through Is get the auditorium. Rs through Zs get the media center. The saggy middle of the alphabet waits for instructions. Finally Js through Qs are packed into a tiny room with four card tables usually reserved for old people who play bridge. I watch as the freshmen and sophomores call their parents and are signed out, one after another, by a young and inexperienced biology teacher. Maybe the principal reasoned that if the upperclassmen found themselves doing the lowerclassmen a favor with the bomb threats, they'd stop.

After they go, attendance is taken, and as soon as the well-meaning biology teacher is out the door, the rest of the Js through Qs up and walk out, leaving just Ethan and me. He looks at me and shrugs. He takes up a worn pack of cards from the basket in the middle of the table where we sit and starts shuffling them.

'Gin?' he asks. 'Canasta? Spit?'

I shake my head. I am eager to have something other than schoolwork to do, but this is not it. There are still some holes in my knowledge normal kids don't have. Most of them were hastily plugged in those first two years thanks to a steady diet of the Disney Channel and the Cartoon Network, but card games I somehow missed.

'No? Okay. How about Crazy Eights?'

I shake my head again. I feel my face getting warm.

'Old Maid? Go Fish?' he asks.

I am trying to think. Do I know any? I watched some kids play at a day camp once.

'Well, what games do you like?'

He is giving me a particular look. Not cruel at all. The opposite, if anything. I've seen it many times before. Curious, maybe a bit searching, like he knows he's pressed against something a little bit tender, and he's promising me he's not going to take advantage of it.

I glance at the shelves, over all the old-people games. I search wishfully for Monopoly. That's the one I know. 'Connect Four.' I can figure that out, right?

'Cards, James. We gotta play cards. I've got it. War,' he says. 'Everyone likes War, right?' He goes ahead and splits the deck and gives half to me. Is he testing me?

I watch him carefully. He puts a card down and I follow. It's clear the person with the higher-number card gets to take the card of the person with the lower one, and also the hierarchy of the cards with the weird-looking royalty on them. I amass a pile, facedown, just like him, of the cards I win.

'War!' he declares when we both put down a card with a four on it.

I look at him expectantly, and he looks at me, and in that split-second delay I realize he knows I don't know how to play War or any of the other games he said.

Deliberately he puts a trail of three cards facedown so I can follow. 'Ready?' he says. 'Last one face up for the win.' He isn't testing me anymore; he is teaching me.

I forget where to put my card. My head is clouding with too many thoughts. Our eyes meet and hold for less than a second.

He knows about me – he doesn't really know, but he knows it's something. Something different, something wrong, and something always afraid. He's known it for a long time. It's what makes me his special case, his charity friend. He knows I can't talk about it, and he's not going to push, but he is going to watch me and try to understand it. These are the moments of clarity between us where I know all this and so does he.

I take off my glasses and rub my eyes. I fumble around with my card. I feel things too much with him.

'Queen!' he cheers me, turning my card over when I finally get it out of my hand. 'Nice!' He'll smooth this over. He'll let me off the hook. He knows I need him to, and he does. 'What a time to pull out the queen, Jamesie. Go ahead and take 'em. They're all yours.' He is happy to have me win. 'I'll get the next one,' he assures me, 'so don't get cocky or anything.'

He is trying to be lighthearted, but his face is also serious, questioning, protective. There's always something under it with us.

'I'm hungry,' he says. 'I've got some change. Let's go buy up the vending machine out front.'

Gratefully, I stand up and follow him, jamming my hands into the front pockets of my jeans.

'Cards weren't taught in a day, you know, Henny,' Ethan says, tapping the deck against my shoulder blade as we walk. 'I think we should start with Go Fish and then maybe Old Maid. Then we'll move on to Spit, and then I think Gin. I've got big plans for you, my friend,' he says.

I don't know what to say. He's accepted this as another of my weird deficits, and he isn't demanding answers; he wants to help. He's found another way in.

'And then, when you are ready, I'm going to teach you the best game of them all . . . Hearts. Trust me, you are going to love it.'

Drip, drip, drip goes the water. I can't keep him out, because I don't want to.

It turns out the vending machine is pretty close to empty when we get there. 'Greedy kids,' Ethan mutters.

'Well, there's chips,' I say, wanting my voice to sound normal.

Ethan makes a face. 'Baked,' he says. 'And what the hell is with the ketchup-flavored chips?'

I laugh. 'Twizzlers?'

'Not greasy enough.'

'The cheese crackers are all broken.'

'They look like they've been there since 1982.'

'Gum won't help anything,' I say.

He sighs. 'What I wouldn't do for three or four of those chocolate cupcakes with the squiggly white icing on top and the fluffy lard inside.'

'There's Fritos,' I say. 'One bag left.'

He nods. 'I guess you're right.' He puts his quarters in the slot and waves his finger over the buttons. 'Uh . . . D . . . uh, four.'

'That's sunflower seeds!' I warn.

'Oh, right. Uh . . . D . . . six.'

'No. Pork rinds!' I shout.

I am laughing. Of course he's messing with me. I

aim my finger at the 5 button and he pulls it away. 'I've got this,' he says, pretending to slip up and hit E3 for Funyuns.

I push his hand away at the last second. 'No one likes those!' I say, like I am your regular, carefree seventeen-year-old girl.

The sound of my laughter shuts me up. I look around for Jeffrey in the direction of the auditorium. Somebody, scold me quick. I am having a bit of a time here.

The Fritos drop from the spiral with a crinkly thump, and Ethan fishes them out.

I excuse myself to go to the bathroom, and I scold myself on the way.

I shouldn't have touched his hand. I shouldn't have laughed. I should not share his Fritos. I lie to myself when I pretend like these things don't mean everything to me.

The phrasing of the twelfth rule is pretty brilliant, in a way. It doesn't say you can't hook up with a time native, though of course that is absolutely forbidden. It doesn't say no kissing or no holding hands or even no to flat-out having sex (unthinkable for so many reasons). Those are the kinds of commands a person could dodge and weave around. Instead, it says you must never be intimate with a time native. That's the kicker. Intimate.

I know what this word means. It is the second's worth of a glance between Ethan and me. It's every time he teases me and I tease him back. It's every nickname he calls me. It's when he taught me how to play War and turned my queen faceup. It is the thing I crave.

And it's the thing they can't quite get me for, because the real proof of it lies inside my head, the only part of me they can't get to.

As it is, I'll get a reprimand when I meet with Mr. Robert next week. I'll say, *Hey, I'm really just trying to act like a regular teenager, that's all it is. And can I help it if I get lumped with Ethan all the time?* They don't want me acting like a recluse or a freak, do they? We can't all be RuneScape addicts like Dexter Harvey, can we?

And once again, if I can sell it well, he'll probably buy it for a little longer, at least. But I do know this: if he or the leaders saw the things I feel in my heart, my face would be up on the screen at the Rules Ceremony next April.

I get back from the bathroom and Ethan is coming toward me with a puzzled look on his face.

'Ben Kenobi is here. I saw him on his way in. He said he's going to be upstairs in the periodicals room and he was hoping to talk to you.'

'Really?' Because this is unusual. Sometimes I leave

the old man cheddar Goldfish or tangerines from the A&P. One cold day I left a hat for him in his shopping cart, but we've never really talked to each other. He's more Ethan's friend than mine. 'Just me?'

'That's what he said.'

I hesitate. I have no reason to be afraid of him. He seems like a sweet man, and very old, and the fact that he drags cans around and is crazy does not prejudice me against him. But still. I go up the steps and Ethan waits for me at the bottom.

The room is dark and otherwise empty, and he is sitting on the floor halfway under a table. He is hard to recognize without his shopping cart and his cans, but I'm sort of touched to see he's got the hat I gave him.

'Will you sit?' he asks me. Most days outside the park, or at the grocery store, his wrinkles seem to angle upward. Today the lines on his face all point down.

I guess he means the floor, so I sit there cross-legged on the overworn brown carpet. I'm glad I left the door partly open.

'Can I look at your glasses?'

Reluctantly, I pass them to him, and the world goes predictably soft. 'I can't see anything without them,' I say.

He examines them and puts them in the hat on his

lap. 'I don't believe that's true,' he says.

'Oh, it's true.'

It's true for all of us immigrants. Something about the passage here did damage to our eyes. Not even contacts can correct it. We all wear specially made glasses to be able to see at all.

'I kind of need those back,' I say, and I wonder, irrationally, if he knows something. The leaders and counselors track our movements, everything we see and say and hear. Nobody says so, naturally, but we all know it's true. I think they do it through our glasses. I think there's got to be a tiny camera and mike planted in them somewhere. Katherine doesn't one hundred percent buy my theory, but while I told her my theory I stuck both pairs of our glasses in my dark closet and shut the door, and Mr. Robert said nothing about it.

'I'll give them back in a minute, but I want to talk to you first.'

I am getting to feel very uneasy. I don't think I've heard him talk before. I am unnerved by the things he's saying, but even more by the sound of his voice. In the low light his hollow cheek glints silver. He's so deeply weathered it's hard to tell how old he is: Seventy? Eighty? Ninety, even? It's especially hard to tell without my glasses.

'Are the glasses that ugly?' I try to say lightly, but he doesn't smile.

'I may need you to help me.'

'Okay,' I say tentatively.

'I don't want to get you involved in this, and if I have a choice, I won't. But just in case I do, I wanted to warn you. Or, I should say, I wanted to ask you.'

My hands are in fists and my fingernails are digging into my palms. He is homeless and he is crazy and it's important for me to be polite.

'Prenna, just listen, because it's important. There is a moment in time when the entire path of the future shifts. It's going to happen soon, and we can't let it pass without doing something.'

My whole body is tingling. My mind is a static mess. The only thoughts I can follow are the most ingrained. *Can Mr. Robert hear what is going on? What rules might I be breaking? How do I disconnect from this situation and yet not bring attention to myself?*

'I am unsure exactly how it will happen,' the old man goes on, serious as a missile. 'But I know *when* it happens. It's less than three weeks away. Nobody sees it coming. It's the kind of juncture you can only see looking back. That's the unnatural privilege we have, you and I, and I am determined to make use of it.'

I start to stand up, but he reaches for my hand. 'Prenna, please. Only another minute. It may be important. There is a single act, a murder, that will change the course of history, and it must be stopped. I don't want to give you any more details if I don't need to.'

The more he talks, the more I feel like I know him. But he's not part of our community. He can't be. His voice digs at my memory. I must have known him from my old life. A friend from my grandmother Tiny's time or maybe an older colleague of one of my parents. I am too panicked to slow my brain down and figure it out.

I picture Mr. Robert. I've got to calm down. I need to play this off. I need to hide my fear. I can't let the old man know any of this is getting to me.

'This man who commits this murder. He told me about it before he died. He was very sick, and he wasn't speaking clearly. But I am sure of the date. I am sure it is the fork, and he knew it too. If we miss it, it's too late. There's no going back.'

'Well.' I clear my throat. I take a breath. I try to sound calm, even patronizing. He is crazy, after all. 'If the guy died, you don't have to worry about him murdering anybody.'

'He's not dead yet,' the old man says, almost impatiently. 'That doesn't happen for another sixty years.'

I feel a new kind of anxiety start at the bottoms of my feet. *Who is he? Where is he from? How does he know these things? Why is he telling this to me?* I caution myself to stop the thoughts in their tracks. Even a broken clock is right twice a day.

'I'm sorry to ambush you like this,' he goes on in a rush. 'I didn't want to, but as I said, I may need your help. We can't let this date pass. Because you know this future almost as well as I do. You know we can't let it happen.'

I get up. I am not calm. I need to get out of here. I don't care how it looks.

'Please. One more thing. Your people say they are doing it, but they are not. They are doing nothing. They are hiding here like cowards, taking what they can for as long as they can.'

I am no longer breathing at all. I don't think my heart is working. I don't say a word.

'This man we're looking for: he doesn't realize what he's doing, but he will in time. By the end, he understood. He said to me before he died, "Please, don't let me do it."'

'I have to go,' I say very, very quietly.

'In case you find yourself in need of help, you can trust your friend Ethan. He sees things other people can't see. He is the one to help you.'

59

I take a step toward the door.

'You know the date already. It's the seventeenth of May. I won't ask for your help unless I have to.'

I stumble out of there as fast as I can, and when I realize what I've done, I stumble back in. 'Please give me back my glasses,' I say. 'I need them.'

He unwraps them from his hat and hands them to me. 'They need you to need them.'

◆ FIVE

I sit in my room and wait for the call. Or the knock. Have they told my mother yet? Will she come home early from work to make sure I do whatever they say? Will it be just Mr. Robert or others too?

It's more than three hours later and my heart still beats wrong. Why hasn't Mr. Robert found me yet?

I have gotten two calls, both from Ethan, but I don't pick up. He's wondering why I ran out of the community center like a lunatic without even signing out, and there's no way I'm going to dodge that without lying.

He sees things other people can't see. What does that mean? Has the old man been feeding the same garbage to Ethan he was trying to feed to me? Ethan would listen gamely. He wouldn't find it troubling the way I do.

I want to seal up everything the man said in a mental

garbage bag and throw it all away at once, but certain sharp things keep poking out.

He made it sound like he came from the same place as me, but that's not possible. He's way too old. He might have already been born here when we came. Talk about straining the integrity of time. Nobody over fifty made the trip.

Of course it's not possible! Why am I even thinking about this? I shout at myself in my head. *He's crazy!*

Why hasn't Mr. Robert contacted me?

Another bit pokes out. The old man said nobody could hear us. He said the thing about them needing me to need my glasses. Did he figure out how to muffle the mike so we couldn't be heard? How could he possibly know about that? He couldn't know about that. So why would he take my glasses? Why would he say that?

And then the very pokiest thing pokes out. He said I know the date. I try not to know the date. I really don't want to know the date.

Slowly and half willingly I let that date turn into numbers. I feel my intestines giving way, a clammy chill overtaking my skin. 51714. I do know the date.

I lie on my bed, trying to fall asleep, imagining why the call and the visit haven't come. It's almost scarier than if they had. I am trying not to think, but I can't, so

I give up and let my mind go where it goes. It keeps going back to the late spring of 2010. There was a strange period of amnesia just before the trip here and just after. I'm not sure why. I guess it's pretty jarring on a body to travel through time. It could have had something to do with the sanitizing process we went through right before we left or the 'vitamins' we took before we set off to reduce the stresses of the trip and protect us against a few dozen common illnesses we were especially vulnerable to.

We still take pills every night to protect us from that stuff, but not nearly as strong. So anyway, I can remember the few days before and then nothing of the actual journey or arrival here.

My first memory in 2010 is the creak of the gate opening to a playground in a place I somehow knew was a few miles and eighty-eight years from home. It was near Rye, in Westchester County, where I waited with a group of adults and about twenty other kids from the immigration for long periods every day those first couple of weeks. It might have been longer or even much shorter. I have no idea how time passed then.

It was during this time that those grown-ups who weren't looking after us got 'situated' – fanning out over the greater New York City area, setting up plausible households and lives for us all.

I remember sitting alone at one end of a seesaw at that playground, facing the wrong direction, obliterated by the over-stimulation of new smells, the sounds, the creatures darting and fluttering around the trees, all those heavy green trees. I remember wondering where my dad was, if maybe he was here with us but so busy making our new life that I hadn't seen him yet.

It was at least a couple of weeks later, probably more – when I moved into our house with my mother and we sat down to our first dinner in this new world – that I realized my father hadn't come and wouldn't come. Mr. Robert and Ms. Cynthia each told me flat-out that my dad had decided at the last minute to abandon the immigration, and I should have accepted it, but it wasn't until that evening that I started to believe it, because my dad hated to miss family dinner.

'Try not to look so stupid,' I remember Ms. Cynthia saying to me sharply in the playground, as I sat slack-jawed and worried on the end of the seesaw.

I imagine now how we must have looked: like a group of refugees from a ragged and wretched place. And we were.

I can remember the clothes I was wearing, picked up for me at some department store along with outfits for all the other kids. We thought they made us fit in, but that's only because we didn't know any better. It was late April and unusually warm, but we wore long sleeves and pants to cover the bruises and cuts from the trip – again, I have no memory of how we got them.

Already, in my very first week here, I was messing up and raising suspicions. The first thing was the dark-blue sweatshirt that said *New York Giants* on it. This was not something we brought with us, but apparently I was found wearing it soon after we arrived. My mom and Ms. Cynthia and Mr. Robert kept asking me where I got it, and I had no idea. Even the great Mrs. Crew took the time to ask me about it. They thought I was lying or hiding something from them, but I wasn't. To this day I cannot tell you how I got it. Honestly, the whole thing is a pure mystery to me.

The fact is, I was supposed to get rid of that sweatshirt, but I still have it folded in a plastic bag on the top shelf of my closet. I'm not sure why I saved it. But I guess that's where my life of private deceit began. Maybe if people accuse you of stuff too much, you figure, you know, might as well.

The second thing was the numbers. I was found wearing a New York Giants sweatshirt from God knows where and with big black numbers scrawled down my arm. Weird kid, I know. I have no idea how that five-digit number got there. Mr. Robert and my mom and the others were upset about that too. I promised I hadn't written it. I think they could tell it wasn't my handwriting. But again, when I had no explanation to offer, they thought I was being difficult.

Mr. Robert was gentle about it, but Ms. Cynthia was downright scary. I can still remember staring at it in shame as she yelled at me, the way the ink bled into the fine texture of my skin. I also remember her scrubbing away at it with the rough side of a sponge until my arm was raw. They kept me in long sleeves and ordered me not to show anyone, but I did show Katherine. And then my mom took up the cause for days after, scouring it in the sink every night until it was finally gone. Those were some stubborn numbers. It's not like I am going to forget them.

December 22, 2011
Dear Julius,

I had another dream about you last night. Maybe because I'm always falling asleep in the middle of writing my letters to you. Because it's late when I write them, and the lights are off and I mostly keep my eyes closed, you know, just in case. No wonder my handwriting sucks! (Sucks = is terrible. You hear that a lot here.)

People use computers. Remember Poppy explained about those? I'm telling you, people here look at them all the time, like they're stuck to one and have no choice. Teachers think it's weird that I like to write everything on pieces of paper. Ms. Scharf said in the future nobody will write anything on paper, and did I want to get left behind?

Yesterday we put lights all over the front of the house and bought a cut-down tree, which we put *inside* the house, and we put lights all over that too. Because of Christmas, which is a really big deal around here. I am not exactly sure what the main idea of it is, and I don't think Mom is either, but that's what all the neighbors are doing.

Mom/Molly gets upset at me for going outside too much. She says kids here don't do that, and it's true. They watch TV or computers or phones or games instead. And not because going outdoors is dangerous or their parents say they can't. They can go out anytime they want. Their parents WANT them to go outside. Staying inside is what they choose.

Love,
Prenna

♦ SIX

As soon as Katherine opens the door the next morning before school, she knows something is up. Her eyes lock on mine, but she can't ask.

I follow her up to her room. Her dad leaves very early for work.

I try to think of a way to couch it. 'You know Ben Kenobi from the A and P?'

'Yeah.'

'He's crazy as a loon.'

'What happened?'

'He was telling me all this stuff about stopping a crime that won't take place until . . . I don't know . . . I forget . . . it was the middle of next month.' I say it as casually as I can, but my eyes tell her to pay attention.

Katherine nods slowly. She knows about the numbers.

I don't know if she'll make the connection. Trying to be subtle, I scratch my arm.

'Of course I got away from him as fast as I could, because he was acting too weird. It's not like I believed anything he said.' I emphasize this for anyone else who might be listening.

I can tell she's calculating. We have a coded way of talking if we need to say things about our parents or our counselors or even about Ethan. I don't have codes for this, but I do say, 'Mr. Fasanelli didn't assign anything for tomorrow,' which more or less means my counselor hasn't said anything yet.

'Well, that's good,' she says.

'Only a matter of time,' I say. 'Might be twice as much work for the weekend.'

The call comes right after school.

'Hey, Mr. Robert,' I say, 'what's up?' My heart is hammering.

'Well, Prenna, I didn't want to wait until our regular meeting to ask you about your conversation with the homeless man you seem to have become friendly with.'

I am scrambling to read his tone. My mom is giving me questioning looks from the kitchen.

'Anything you're concerned about?' he asks.

I used to like Mr. Robert. I was so happy when I got

assigned to him and not to Ms. Cynthia. He has a round, friendly face, and he always used to wear a tie with rainbows or frogs or something to amuse me. He makes his questions sound like he's trying to take care of you.

'Not really,' I say. 'I mean, he's crazy. I didn't realize how crazy, so that's kind of sad.'

'Yes, it is.' I can hear that Mr. Robert wants more.

'It made me pretty uncomfortable, to tell you the truth,' I say solemnly.

'That must have been hard for you.' I can picture his face perfectly as he says this. He is frowning in his patronizing way. Maybe he is rubbing his fat chin, full of concern. He was Aaron Green's counselor too. He probably used to say things like this to Aaron. But it was long before Aaron's death that I had stopped trusting Mr. Robert to actually care about me. I guess overhearing his crisp, all-business approach to the disposal of my dead body had had something to do with it.

'I mean, you know me,' I say cheerfully. 'I'm always trying to be attentive to people. I think that's important, and we've talked about that a lot, but I don't think it makes sense for me to be friendly with him anymore.' I sound so phony I could throw up, but mercifully Mr. Robert is obtuse. They taught us to be great liars. So what do they expect?

71

'I think that's wise, Prenna.'

He says that a lot. I used to think he simply meant I was being wise. By now I know he means *If we find you talking to that man again, you will be sorry.*

After school the next day I ask Katherine to come swimming with me at the indoor pool at the Y.

On account of us being obliged to act like normal girls, and not do weird things like swim laps at the Y with our custom-made glasses on, I have taken to swimming when I want to talk honestly with Katherine. Mr. Robert must suspect what I am up to, because the last two times Katherine and I went swimming we both got reprimanded. But the real takeaway for me was that he didn't mention any of the things Katherine and I had talked about – and I had tossed out a few highly controversial tidbits just to test the theory. We'll get reprimanded this time for sure, and maybe even punished. Last time, Mr. Robert couldn't come up with a convincing reason to ban swimming in a pool, but he's probably come up with one by now. It may be the last time we are able to get away with it, but I take the risk anyway.

'I can't stop thinking about the number,' I tell her once we're paddling in the deep middle of the underheated pool.

Katherine nods. Without my glasses my vision is so poor that she's not much more than shapes and colors, but I can tell her lips are a little blue. 'I didn't get it at first, but I do now,' she says carefully.

'All this time I've been trying to figure it out and I never thought it was a date. Now I can't think of it any other way.'

She's afraid to talk. I can tell. This is dangerous, and, as I said, she isn't one hundred percent sold on my glasses theory.

So I hurry ahead. I say the thing I shouldn't say and shouldn't even think: 'What if he's not crazy? Or at least, not crazy about everything? What if this date is real and there is something he needs me to do?'

Katherine nods again. I know her expression without being able to see it very well. Her green-brown eyes are wide open with worry for me.

'Should I talk to him? I know I am not supposed to, but what if he contacts me again? I can't just let this date come and go and not do anything, can I? He says our people aren't fixing anything, just hiding. I am so afraid that is true.'

Katherine's alarm, even blurry, is hard to ignore.

'I'm sorry,' I say. 'I'll stop. I shouldn't involve you in it. I accept getting myself in trouble, but I don't want to do it to you. I will shut up now.'

'I don't mind. It's just I am worried for you,' she says in barely a whisper. 'That's all. Please, please be careful.'

I paddle around in circles, trying to get warm. 'I think I have to talk to him,' I say. I am terrible at shutting up.

February 12, 2011
Dear Julius,

You just can't believe the stuff they have here. There is this place called "the mall" where they've kind of walled in a whole town of different stores, some of them as big as canyons, where they sell millions and millions of things, way more than people can even buy. Not because they CAN'T buy them, usually, but because they already have so much stuff in their houses that they don't need them. When the mall closes at night, there's still practically as much stuff left to buy as there was in the morning when it opened. People don't rush around or line up in giant queues as you might expect. It's just normal here to have all this extra stuff around that you DO NOT EVEN NEED.

I'm not sure where it all comes from, because you never see anybody making anything.

Love,
Prenna

SEVEN

Every day after school for a week I walk through the park and then past the A&P. I haven't decided for sure what to do about the old man yet. As I try on the idea that he might know what he's talking about, I can't help having all these questions. For now I just want to see him. I even try the community center again, but he's not in any of these places.

'Have you seen Ben Kenobi lately?' Ethan asks me on Monday at the end of the school day, taking the thought straight out of my brain.

I've been avoiding Ethan since the incident at the community center. I don't want him to ask me why the old man wanted to talk to me or what he said. Ethan seems to understand this. But now he's standing at my locker, chewing gum.

'No. Not in a few days.' I put my history textbook in my backpack. I clear my throat. I can't let anything lie. 'Why?'

'I have something I want to give him. There's this paper a scientist wrote at the place I interned last summer. I think he would find it really interesting.'

Something in Ethan's manner seems a little artificial to me, a little manic, and it's not just the gum.

I'm not sure what to say to this. There is rarely an unwanted silence between Ethan and me; we can usually fall back on banter. But today we stare at each other. Neither of us quite knows what to do about it.

So he keeps talking. 'She's brilliant, this woman who wrote the paper. She's just come out of MIT in physics, doing this work on traversable wormholes that is just wild. Her real field is wave energy, so this is like her hobby.' He pulls the paper out of his book bag and hands it to me. It is full of diagrams and equations.

'You can read this?'

'Mostly.' He looks up, realizing he's forgotten to be the guy who needs help on his physics problem sets. He finds a wrapper in his pocket and spits his gum into it. 'I mean, not all of it, obviously. But I've been fascinated by this stuff since I was, like, thirteen years old, since I had this . . . well . . .' He stops and looks at me.

He opens his mouth and closes it.

'Since what?'

'Since I . . . Nothing. Never mind.' Ethan's forehead is crimping with agitation.

It's always me who's cautious, me who's secretive, me who talks myself into corners. Very strange to see Ethan acting this way. Frankly, I think I do a better job with it.

'Since you what?' I probably shouldn't ask. The counselors are probably tuning in to everything I say and do right now exactly as I say and do it.

Ethan is eyeing me carefully. 'It's just that I had this very strange experience when I was thirteen. I went fishing at this creek not far from my house . . .' His expression is bewildering to me, just as it was the first time I talked to him. Like he's looking to me for some kind of understanding.

'Yeah?' Suddenly I am wondering why, if this is so important, he never told me about it before, and why he is telling me now.

'I don't really talk about it much. I mean, I told my folks at the time and they had no idea what to make of it. I made some drawings to show them, and they made an appointment to show *me* to the school shrink.' He laughs, but it doesn't seem to strike either of us as funny.

Slowly the hubbub in the hallway is dying down, and

now it's quiet enough to measure the full weirdness between us.

'I told Mona – Dr. Ghali – the physicist I was talking about. And actually, I told Ben Kenobi. I showed him drawings. He's the one who, well, anyway . . .'

'Ethan, *what*? What happened?' I am getting nervous and impatient. I don't know where this is going, what it has to do with me, or just how much trouble I am potentially getting us into, and yet I can't seem to hold back.

'Just this strange kind of . . . disturbance in the air over the river. Really hard to describe, and then . . .' Still that searching look.

'What?'

He shakes his head. He looks tired and uncertain. 'You really don't remember, do you?'

Mr. Robert calls twice before dinner and I don't pick up. This is not okay. The cell phone I carry is for his convenience more than mine, though he would never say so. You can sometimes get away with a couple of standard excuses: I'm so sorry – I lost my charger and now my phone is dead. OMG, my phone didn't even ring, isn't that weird? But I am at the very outer limit.

I go over to Katherine's house right after dinner. My

mom gives me a heavy look as I walk out the door. The windows at Katherine's house are dark. Katherine and her dad aren't go-out-at-night people. I try to think of comforting excuses on the way home. It's not curriculum night or college night or science social night at school, is it? Could be, right?

'Mr. Robert called,' my mother tells me as soon as I walk in the door.

'I misplaced my phone,' I say lightly. 'I must have left it in my locker at school.'

'Make sure you get it tomorrow,' she warns me.

'I will.'

'He wants you to stay put for the rest of the evening and come home directly after school tomorrow, and I assured him you would. He said he'd be in touch about speaking in person before your next scheduled session.'

I am already halfway up the stairs.

'Prenna?'

'Uh-huh?'

'Everything okay?'

I need to say something. She needs to feel like she's doing her job. 'The homeless guy from the parking lot at the A&P said a bunch of weird stuff to me because he's crazy, and Mr. Robert wants to follow up. That's all.'

Later on I sort of, oops, drop my phone out the back

window of my house. Before I do, I make sure it's not supposed to rain. It lands among the daffodils that I myself planted. Now my phone really is misplaced. Darn.

I think about what Ethan said. I try his words a hundred different ways. A thousand. There is no way I am going to sleep tonight.

Katherine is not in school the next day. I am starting to panic. What am I going to do? I am in agony. I wait by Katherine's locker between every class, hoping I am wrong. Hoping she'll show up. Maybe she just had a sore throat or something.

I can't stand the idea of going home after school, especially because of being ordered to. It occurs to me: I could wait for Mr. Robert to find me, or I could go find him.

He's not at his office the first time I check. The second time he is.

'Prenna. Just the girl I've been trying to reach,' Mr. Robert says, opening the door for me.

Without thinking, I go and plant myself on his couch as I've done for the last four years. 'Where is Katherine Wand?'

He sits down and creaks around in his swivelly office

chair. He adjusts his glasses, no hurry at all. 'Katherine has decided to complete the semester at a terrific boarding school in New Hampshire.'

I glower at him. '*Katherine* has decided?'

'Please watch your tone, Prenna.'

I take a deep breath. 'Why did she decide that?'

'Frankly, Cynthia and her father encouraged her,' Mr. Robert says evenly. 'Among other things, we felt perhaps the two of you needed a break. I think you are putting her in a difficult position, discussing inappropriate subjects with her and demanding her secrecy. She is very loyal to you.'

I am translating as he goes: they wanted information from her and she wouldn't tell them, so they sent her away. It's almost certainly not to a terrific boarding school, but it's probably some measure short of actually harming her. Probably a community safe house. At least, I pray it is. It may or may not be in New Hampshire.

'Katherine didn't do anything wrong. Why are you punishing her?'

He creaks back in his chair and crosses his arms over his fat stomach. He, like a lot of the adults in our community, has taken a bit too much advantage of the abundance of easy food they've got here.

'We're not viewing this as a punishment, Prenna. This

is an opportunity to take her out of a difficult and possibly compromising situation.'

Blah, blah, blah. What I'm wondering is, why don't they send me away? If it suited their purposes, they would put me away in a second. They'd give my mom the same lame-ass story about the terrific boarding school, and she would support them, no problem.

'Let us spend a moment talking about your friend Ethan,' Mr. Robert says, exactly as expected.

'Okay.'

'The conversation you had at the end of the school day yesterday.'

I shrug. 'Yeah.'

'Do you know what he was getting at?'

I look straight at him. It's nice to take a brief vacation from lying. 'Not at all.'

'Do you understand why he was discussing it with you?'

I shrug again. 'I guess because of being in physics together.'

I stare into the bowl of jelly beans he keeps on his coffee table. I used to eat them by the handful until the time I got pneumonia, and I haven't eaten one since.

Then it dawns on me: maybe they are letting me stumble around for a while longer because they want to know what I might find out.

'You know that old homeless man we were talking about before?' I say. I sound combative to my own ears. I am sure anyone listening to me right now would wish I would shut up. I know I wish I would.

'Of course.'

'He says we're not doing anything to prevent the plagues or make anything better at all. He says we're just hiding out here.' I want to get a rise out of him, but Mr. Robert is pretty good at controlling his expression.

'And you believe what he said?'

'No. I don't know. I don't think so. But even if he's crazy, is it possible he knows something?'

'Do you think that?'

'No,' I say with more conviction this time. 'But it made me think about it. So are we doing anything? What are we doing?'

Now he's leaning back with his arms up and his head resting in his hands. I am looking into his armpits.

'Prenna, you need to trust that we are doing what is best for the community and for the world. But as you well know, we need to operate within the rules. When you are a little older, and if you can prove you are capable of observing those rules with absolute strictness and discretion, you will take your part in our efforts.'

I basically tune out everything he says after my name. Whenever he starts a sentence with my name, I know he's lying. Whenever he starts a sentence with a word other than my name, I know he's lying.

'Right, Mr. Robert. I understand,' I say.

And as he drones on about the deep importance of trust, I sit there gazing at the jelly beans and finally coming to terms with a deep and basic conflict: How can you fix anything if you can't change anything?

Mr. Robert won't get anywhere with me and I won't get anywhere with him. But if he's giving me the latitude to gather some information, maybe I should gather information until someone stops me.

He looks at his watch. 'All right, Prenna. Take your pills, stay healthy, be good.' He always says some version of that when it's time for me to go.

He stands; I stand. I frown at him. 'You should bring Katherine home and send me instead.'

He loosens his shamrock tie. He's had about enough of me. 'Don't tempt me, Prenna.'

I retrieve my phone from the daffodils and walk to the park as evening falls over my neighborhood. I pause for that moment when all the street and sidewalk lights come on at once. Then I keep going. I go to the picnic table where the old man is most likely to be perched with his cart and his cans and his grimy peacock feathers, but he's not there.

I sit by myself and check my phone. A missed call from an unfamiliar number and three voice mail messages from Mr. Robert. I delete the messages without listening. For no good reason I call Katherine's number. There is no way she's going to pick it up. I'm sure she's got another number by now, if she has any phone at all. I hear her sweet whispery voice on her outgoing message. I call again and listen again, and then I start to cry. I lie back on the picnic table and watch the leaves moving like a veil of black lace over the deep evening sky.

My mind goes to Aaron Green. He tried to make it here. He really did.

I don't want to end up like that. None of us is remotely free, but at least I get to walk in the sunshine and grow flowers, eat raspberries and swim in the ocean sometimes.

There is no way they can do that to Katherine. I won't let it happen. I will never tell her another thing if it means she can come home.

◆ EIGHT

'I trust you are using earphones to listen to this message.'

The mysterious number came up on my phone while I was standing in the kitchen. I ran up to my room before I played the new message. Now I push the button on my phone to pause the old man's voice. My heart is galloping. I check the hallway, listening for my mother's voice downstairs. I close the door of my room very quietly and stuff the earbuds a little tighter in my ears. It's hard to say this man doesn't know what he's talking about. I sit down on my bed and push the button to resume.

'I hope I haven't scared you,' he says. 'I know you have trouble believing what I've said. That is natural. But I hope you'll think it through and trust your reason. Your people weren't the only travelers to use the time path. I came alone, twenty-four years after you, but I arrived in the same place at the same time. I know what you went through. I went through it too, and more. I know Katherine is gone, Prenna, and you must be feeling alone. I encourage you, whatever happens, to talk to Ethan and tell him the truth. He already knows more than you realize. In the meantime, there is something I would like to give you . . . just in case. Come find me when you can. And, Prenna, take off those glasses they've got you wearing, go get those pills they've got you taking, and throw them all in the garbage.'

How can he expect me to do these things? Does he not know about the rules? Does he not realize that my community, my past and my continued existence hang in the balance? It's not like there's some other life I can choose.

I listen to the message twice more before I delete it. There's that strange pull in his voice. I want to fit him into some memory of my old life and I'm also scared to try. It was so long since we were there, and the atmosphere of my life was so different then, it feels impossible to extend any clear memory from that time to this one. It feels like they took place in different languages and there is no code to translate between them.

And there's that irrational hope, the tormenting spark that's kept me searching from the day we got here, sent me following a stranger in a plaid vest. I've given up so many times, I don't think I can try again. But what if?

He says to tell Ethan the truth. I try picturing it. I try to think of the words I would say: *Ethan, I am from the future.* Really?

I don't think I could do it. If Mr. Robert called and told me to, I don't know if I could do it. It would be like peeing in my pants in the middle of assembly. It goes so hard against everything I know, I'm not sure I could physically do it.

And how could I possibly ditch my glasses and my pills? Does the man want me to die? If so, there are easier and faster ways to kill me. If I do any part of what he says, I will set them in motion.

How can I trust him? Who trusts the homeless, can-collecting man who sings opera to himself? Who does that?

Something about the way he said my name. *What if . . . ?*

He said to trust my reason. Well, my reason tells me not to do those things he says.

I won't do those things.

In the meantime, I find the number he called from and call it back. It's an impersonal, computer-voiced message – the kind that comes when you buy the phone.

I tap my foot, waiting for the beep.

'There are rules I have to follow,' I say. 'I won't survive if I break them.'

After dinner I see I have a message from the same number. I shut myself in my closet with my earbuds.

'Time has her rules, Prenna. I won't argue that. The real ones are inescapable – you can't break them if you try. And you will learn, maybe painfully, what they are.

'Many of the rules you've been taught are just for the sake of controlling and dominating you. But not all of them are wrong. You must be careful. We are interlopers here, and we must be humble and cautious. We can do terrible damage – it's possible we already have. There are ramifications to everything we do. Some we hope will be good. But we should not interfere with time's sequence more than we have to.

'I wish you could have everything you could want in this life, Prenna, but I fear there are limits to what we can ask for.'

I hang up. I stare at my phone. I have that thought: *What if?*

I have another thought: *What did any of that mean?*

After a while I have a third thought. I open my window and throw my phone back into the daffodils.

June 2012

Dear Julius,

I ate mango. It's a sticky orange fruit, sweet and sour, and it comes apart in threads, with a hard little skull in the middle of it. It is so good. Even better than pineapple. I think I would eat it even if you told me it was deadly poisonous.

I keep thinking that when the time comes around for you to be born, we are going to have fixed the world so there will still be mango. Just picturing you taking one bite, Julius. That makes everything worth it.

Love,
Prenna

◆ NINE

At school I am practically jumping out of my skin, knowing where I am going after the last bell and knowing the first question I'm going to ask when I get there.

Ethan keeps trying to approach me, and I avoid him. At the beginning of math class he plunks a gift down on my desk. I glance at the door. Mr. Fasanelli is late; there's no getting out of this. I stare at his offering. The gift-wrapping job is so poor, I am sure he's done it himself.

'Should I open it now?' I ask.

'Sure,' he says.

'Nice wrapping,' I say.

He shrugs, not sure whether I am serious. 'I used too much tape,' he says.

It is a brand-new pack of cards, still in its cellophane. I knock them against my palm, enjoying the density of them, appreciating the hokey image of water lilies on the back.

'Thanks,' I say.

He nods, and by his face I know he is trying to say something with them. *I'll play along*, he is saying. *I'll teach but I won't ask.*

And here, I realize, is a thing you can't undo. When you open yourself to somebody, when you feel these things that you feel, well, what do you do then? You can try to ignore it, maybe you can try to forget about it, but you can't undo it and you can't give it back.

'Are you . . . ?'

    'Have you . . . ?'

    'Did you . . . ?'

    'Am I . . . ?'

This is a difficult question to phrase. But I have to ask him. There are so many other questions that would naturally ensue. But this is the first and the hardest.

I am walking in my reverie when I discover that Ethan is behind me, hurrying to catch up.

'Why are you following me?' I ask.

'Can I talk to you for a minute?'

'Can't we talk later?'

'Can we talk now? It's kind of important.' He doesn't

seem to care that I am walking briskly away from him.

'Later?'

'Now?'

'I can't now.' I say that, but I stop. I can't ignore him. I can't intentionally hurt him.

'Prenna, I know there is a lot of stuff you don't want to talk about, like where you come from. Maybe you think you can't tell me. And that's fine. You don't have to say anything you don't want to say, but the thing is . . .'

I start walking again. I can't afford to destroy myself. Not yet.

'The thing is . . .'

I turn a corner. I am practically running.

'The thing is, I think I already know.' Ethan's eyes, when I hazard a glance at them, are begging me to talk to him.

If any of the natives know the truth about you – any of them! – no matter how helpful and kind they might appear, they will take you apart. They might act like they want to help, but they won't. They will destroy you and destroy all of us.

These are the teaching words from my mother, from Mr. Robert, from my friends, from every person I know and count on.

I am starting to slow down. I don't know how long I can run from this. 'And why is that?'

'Because a few days ago Ben Kenobi told me. And he said—'

I turn on him. 'Have you not noticed that he is crazy?'

'I've talked to him a lot. I don't think he's crazy.'

'Really?' I'm performing now, and I'm not very good at it.

'Really.'

'And what did he tell you?' I try to sound sarcastic and unconcerned, but it's not coming out right.

Ethan is being careful. He gives me a questioning look. To my astonishment he reaches out and takes my glasses from my face. He puts them in his back pocket. When he speaks again, his voice is slow and quiet. 'He told me you are not from a different place.' He is talking so slowly I can hear my own fast breathing between each word. 'You're from a different time.'

I gape at him. I feel myself deflating. I feel too tired to lift my head. Now what? I need to be amazed by the absurdity of this. Such preposterousness knows no bounds! I need to puff up. I wish I could. 'And you are going to believe that because a homeless man who wears peacock feathers told you?' I gesture weakly toward his back pocket. 'And he also told you they monitor us with the glasses?'

Ethan is silent, and I feel a compulsive, panicky energy building, a need to fill the air with words. 'If he's Ben Kenobi, are you supposed to be Luke Skywalker? Am I supposed to be Princess Leia? Or are you seeing me more like one of the weird guys in the alien bar?' I think I'm trying to be funny, but no one is laughing.

Ethan looks hurt. He deserves some honesty from me, but he's not getting it. We are deep in rule-breaking territory here, and I need to be careful.

'I won't believe him if you tell me not to,' he says, again so quietly I can barely hear. His eyes are locked on mine. He always sees more than he should see.

Now is my opening, my opportunity to do the thing I was taught to do above all other things: to tell the lie and tell it well. Instead, I am struck dumb, my eyes filling with tears. What a failure I am. I don't tell the lie or tell it well. I just stand there like an idiot.

'Oh, Prenna.' He sees my tears. I know he doesn't want to hurt me. Whatever they say.

I think I could lie to anyone else in the world right now. I think I could lie in rhyming verse to Mr. Robert or Jeffrey Boland or even my mother. I could lie in perfect sonnets to Ms. Cynthia or Mrs. Crew. But I look at his face and I can't lie to Ethan.

He starts to reach for me, but I wipe at my eyes and turn sharply in the opposite direction. 'I have to go,' I say.

'We haven't got much time,' he says to me as I walk away.

It's less than half a block before I realize it's not just the tears blinding me. I strode away without my glasses, and I can't go back. I'm too proud, too afraid, too determined, and, as the counselors are fond of reminding me, too stupid.

I wait for the old man in the park. I think he'll be there because it's quieter and more private than the grocery store parking lot, and I'm not sure where else he has to go. I sit at the picnic table next to his favorite clearing. I stumble around the perimeter of the park a couple of times just in case.

I have some time to think about his life, the places he goes, the things he carries. Little by little I let my mind run over the things he said and tentatively follow the possibility that some of them are true. I try them out, like plugging new variables into a very complicated equation and seeing how it holds together.

The truth is strong. Unlike a lie, it gets stronger over time, and it has the power to draw disparate feelings and ideas together in a way that a lie never can. The more I think about the things he said, the more I can sense the power of truth in them.

The less crazy I imagine him, the more tragic he seems.

And the *what if* . . . I can't think my way into the *what if*, because even a tiny step stings me with hope and fear and drags along behind it a feeling that is overwhelmingly sad.

I slow down long enough to wonder about Ethan too. What should I do? It's an unthinkable sin to tell an outsider our secret. But what if that outsider already knows?

A couple of hours pass, and it's getting dark. I've been perched in such an odd position both my feet have fallen asleep. It's time to shake them out and be on my way. I'll try the parking lot. That's the place where I've left things for him in the past. Maybe that's where he expects me to look.

I can't think very far ahead. I really can't see very far ahead. I can't go home and face my mother and Mr. Robert. I can only think of finding Ben Kenobi, discovering what he has for me and asking the question I have to ask.

I scan the parking lot very carefully in small sections. I see no sign of him in the front part of the lot, so I go around the side of the giant store. It is quiet here now. Very few cars even in the best spots. The sides and the back will be empty.

I hear something. Kind of a guttural sound, and it scares me. It's not a good sound. It comes from the back of the lot. I hear it again and then a shout that doesn't form a word.

I am running now. Putting my arms out, I am guided by my ears more than my eyes. I run toward the sound. There is little light back there, but I see shapes and shadows moving and hear a voice crying out.

'Who's there?' I scream.

As I get close I see the outline of a figure bent over. It's a man, I'm almost sure, not tall but thickly built. I make out the brim of a baseball cap on his head. He stops and turns for a moment. Does he see me? I think he must, because he stands up and runs across the lot and disappears around the side of the store. If my eyes were better, if the light were better, I would have been able to see his face.

There is another shape, which is a shopping cart, and

a darker shape, which is on the ground. I go down on my knees, putting my hands on that dark shape. I hear the moans. I feel the warm wetness across his chest I know is blood. I know who it is.

I pull the old man onto my lap. I lean very close to see his face. He's breathing roughly, choking on blood. His neck is cut. Who knows what else.

'Prenna.'

He looks up at me, and of course it is him. Of course. I lean close and put my cheek on his. 'It's me.'

His eyes are his eyes again, full of clarity, though it's a struggle to talk. 'You know . . .'

I don't want him to have to struggle. 'I know.'

'I didn't want to . . . put you in this . . .'

I put my arms around him. 'It's okay. I understand. I think I understand now.'

His eyes close and then flutter open for a second.

'I will take care of it,' I say into his ear. 'I will make sure.' I know this is what comforts him. I feel his body loosen in my arms. I don't know what I'm promising, but I know I mean it.

His eyes close again. I hear the last sounds going out of him, feel the last of his warmth mixing into the air.

I hear footsteps coming, but I can't move. I can't pull away and leave him. I don't care what happens to me.

'Oh, God.'

I look up at the sound of Ethan's voice.

I feel his hand on my back. 'Oh, Prenna.'

I can't let the old man go.

'Is he dead?'

'Just . . . Yes.'

'Did you see what happened?'

It takes me a little while to find my voice. I choke on words like my throat was cut too. 'I came at the end. I didn't see who it was. He ran away.'

He's wrapped both arms around me. 'You can't stay here,' he says gently. 'We have to go.'

'I can't.'

'You have to.' He lets go of me and goes over to the cart. He sifts through it and picks out an envelope and stuffs it in his jacket. He comes back to me and helps me lay the old man down carefully. He lifts me up. I'm sobbing. I hear myself sobbing. I guess that must be me.

I don't fight him. I let him carry me along like I'm a baby. He puts me in his car and closes the door. He drives out of the lot and away from the store. He scans the long blocks and finally finds a pay phone along a deserted stretch. I understand that he calls 911.

Back in the car, he drives onto the highway for a couple of miles and then back off the highway onto smaller and smaller roads. Finally he stops the car on a remote street. He kills the engine and reaches for me. He pulls me toward him so I'm nearly in his lap and holds me with both arms. He strokes my hair and wipes away my tears. We just stay like that for a long time.

◆ TEN

'You know, right?' he says to me after the tears are through.

I've sat up and retaken my own seat. He's still holding my hands. In the midst of everything are dull alarms in my head that I could be hurting him by being close like this. And there's the blood drying all down my front and on my arms and hands. It's on him too. It doesn't seem to scare him and it doesn't scare me. I've seen death before. I've seen plenty of blood before. I've seen suicide and I've even seen murder. But it horrifies me to know whose it is. And I do know, though I can't yet put my Poppy and this poor old man together into the same person.

I nod. I guess that means he knows too.

'I'm sorry.'

'For both of us,' I say.

'For both of us.'

'I wish I could have talked to him . . . you know, knowing.' It seems unfair to discover your father is alive at the same moment he is dying.

'Him too.'

I try to take it in slowly. It's too much at once and I'm worried I'll just shut down. Sometimes I think our minds have an immune system, just like our bodies do, but you have to give it time to work.

'How long have you known?' I ask.

'Not long. Couple of weeks.'

'You've been trying to tell me.'

'I guess. I've been wanting to tell you a lot of things, but I didn't know how. It's a lot to lay on a person. And I know you're not supposed to talk to me. Not really talk.'

I nod. I can still feel my cheek against the old man's cheek. 'I think at the end we both knew everything.'

'That's good. And that you were there.'

'I wish I'd gotten to him sooner.' I think of something. 'What made you come?'

'He called me twice. The second time I just heard a lot of shouting. I knew something was wrong.'

'Do you think he knew this was going to happen?'

'He might have. He just wanted to make it another few days, but he knew somebody was watching him. I've been worried. I've been worried for both of you.'

I don't know how to keep pretending. I didn't tell Ethan the truth about me, but I didn't deny it either. I don't know how much he knows.

The strange thing is, I think I'm keeping all these secrets from him, but he seems to know more than I do. He's full of certainty and I'm not sure of anything anymore. I can't keep straight what is supposed to be true and what is true, they are diverging so quickly.

'They are going to come for me, you know,' I say quietly.

He nods.

'Where are my glasses?'

'I wore them at home and left them in the trunk of my father's car before he went to play squash in Spring Valley. I am hoping that might confuse things a little.'

I consider this. I almost smile at the picture in my mind. 'So you think they can't hear us or see us now? You think the glasses are their only way?'

'Kenobi—' He breaks off and reconsiders the name.

'You can call him Kenobi,' I say. I'm too distraught, too disoriented to call him by his name.

'That's what he thought.'

I put my hand over a spot of blood drying into the knee of my pants. 'I've suspected it was the glasses for a long time. It makes sense. We're all blind and defenseless without them.'

'You don't have to be.'

'What do you mean?'

'He said they've got you all taking these pills. They say it's to build your immune system or something, but all they really do is ruin your vision and make it so nobody has kids. He thinks – he thought – if you stop taking them, your sight will come back.'

How can I believe that? I pull my hands back from him. My mother is part of the medical clinic that issues the pills. She wouldn't let them do that. Another version of my life is shifting and reshaping behind me.

'What about your phone?'

'I threw it out the window.' I shake my head, trying to think. 'But, Ethan, what if he's wrong about the pills?'

'Do you have any of them with you?'

'No.'

'Then let's hope he's right.'

'Why do you say that?'

'Because we can't go back for them. We've only got three days. We've got to get moving.'

I stare at him. I feel more tears seeping into my eyes.

'Do you really think it's that easy? That I can just get away from them and off we go?'

'For a few days we can. That's what Kenobi thought. He said they would kill you if they had no other choice, but I won't let them. He says their power has limits. They are omnipotent in your world, but not in mine. And all we need are a few days. Then everything will be different. After that I'll talk to them if you want.'

I stare at him in stupefaction. I can hear Ms. Cynthia telling me to shut my mouth and to try not to look like an idiot. 'That shows you really don't know anything.'

'Maybe not. We'll see.'

'You literally believe everything he said?'

'I do.'

'Why?'

'Because I've seen some strange things in my life.' I can feel his eyes fixed on mine. 'They never made sense, but I couldn't ignore them. What he said fits with what I've seen.'

'Maybe you're both crazy.'

He shrugs. He doesn't look particularly concerned by that idea. 'Maybe so. I'll consider that next week. For the moment I'm going with what he said. For the next few days, anyway.'

'Because of May seventeenth.'

For the first time some relief creeps into his eyes. He lets out a breath. 'Yes, because of May seventeenth.'

We are quiet for a moment.

'I can't tell you how long I've been trying to figure out the meaning of that number,' he says.

The way he looks at me is making me dizzy. 'Because he told it to you?'

'Way before that. Because I saw it on your arm.'

I close my eyes. 'How?'

He moves closer to me. He takes my hands again. He unbends my left arm and pushes up my sleeve and runs his fingers over the place where it was.

I shiver. My skin holds the memory of the rawness from all the scrubbing.

'I saw you four years ago. I think it was when you first got here. You were like the girl in the Robert Burns poem: wet and draggled, coming through the rye. I was thirteen, and I was fishing by myself for the first time at Haverstraw Creek. There had been this crazy disturbance in the air over the stream. It was the most incredible thing I've ever seen. Ben Kenobi says that it was one end of the time path. That's where you all came through.'

I can't stop shaking. 'I don't remember.'

'I know. I realize that. You were in bad shape. You

were cold and alone and you had the number scrawled on your arm. I wanted to help you. I gave you my sweatshirt—'

I spin. I float. I try to breathe. 'That was you.' *Of course.*

Now I think, *Of course.*

'The air around you was quivering in the strangest way. You were scared and you didn't want to talk to me. I pointed the way to a bridge over the river, where you thought you needed to go.'

'I don't remember any of it,' I say faintly. Again I feel the world shifting and reshaping behind me. 'Did you see other people besides me?'

'No. They were probably coming into the woods in other places. I only saw you.' I can't see his expression well enough to read it, but I sense he is weighing his words. 'But I can recognize them – the people who came. Some easier than others.'

'What do you mean?'

'I can recognize travelers. It's hard to describe. It's like the air moves around you in a slightly different way. Not like on the day you came, but a very, very subtle version of it.'

'You can see that right now?'

'On you, barely. Almost not at all anymore. But on

others more, particularly the older ones. I could see it pretty strongly on Kenobi.'

'Can other people see it?'

'Nobody I've ever met. Not that I talk to people about it a lot. Kenobi says it's rare, but some people have an acute sensitivity to the time stream. Maybe because I was there that day when the path opened. Some effects of the stream are always there, but most people don't see it. He says it's like that psychological experiment everybody watches on YouTube. With the people throwing the basketball? You've probably seen it.'

I shake my head.

'Okay, so there are two basketball teams, one wearing black shorts, the other white. You are supposed to count the number of times the white team throws the basketball to the black team and vice versa. At the end they tell you the answer, and then they ask: Did you see the gorilla?'

'The gorilla?'

'Yeah. The majority of people are so occupied by counting the throws, they don't see that a guy in a gorilla suit walks right into the middle of the court while the players are throwing the ball, stands there, and then walks away. Most people have no idea the gorilla was there.'

I edge closer to him. I hold his hand. 'You see the gorilla.' His voice sounds tired, and for the first time I can tell that he is sad. 'I guess I do.'

Ethan fumbles in his jacket and presents me with the envelope he took from the old man's shopping cart.

'Is this what he wanted to give me?'

'He said that he had something for you – a key – but that if for any reason he couldn't give it to you himself, I should find this and make sure to put it in your hands. I think it's lucky you didn't give his murderer more time to look around.'

I realize that is true.

'Are you going to open it now?' he asks as I knead the envelope in my hands. I find myself feeling it, shaking it like it is a Christmas present, wanting to even out the shocks if I can. There's a letter inside. A key jiggles at the bottom. That's the thing he wanted to make sure I got one way or another.

Ethan turns the car key halfway in the ignition to put the interior lights on. 'You ready?'

'You'll have to read it to me,' I say.

Along with the key and the letter is a small piece of paper with an address wrapped around a magnetized plastic card. Ethan reads the writing on the card:

Secure Storage
200 East 139th Street
Bronx, NY 10451

That's what the key is for.

I open the letter and squint down hard over the writing. The shape of it. The shape of the signature at the bottom. Blind though I am, the writing stirs more feelings in me. I close my eyes. 'Okay. Read,' I say.

My dear Prenna,

If you are reading this letter, then my fears have been realized. I've been being followed for some time now, and I know my life is in danger. I wouldn't have reached out to you at all if I could have avoided it. I hate the thought of putting you in harm's way. But, again, if you are reading this, I need your help.

I am your father; you are my daughter. Maybe you know it already.

I am hideously changed. I have aged almost twenty-four years while you and the other travelers have aged only four. I stayed much longer in an inhospitable world before I could get back here.

I know they told you I abandoned the immigration, but I didn't. I never by choice would have let you and your mother go without me. I disagreed with some of the other leaders about the goal of our undertaking. I know the rules as well as anybody, and the danger of uncontainable changes, but some changes – even if it's just one critical change – must be made. Otherwise, we know how it ends. I wasn't the only one who believed this, but I suppose I was the most strident. I was the only one left behind. The rest of them, including your mother, made the trip but were stripped of any power, any say, in how the community operates.

You must wonder as you read this why I've lived the way I've lived, and I don't know if I can explain myself adequately. I've been on the streets and in the park not because I lacked access to money or shelter, but because my shopping cart and sleeping bag and peacock feathers are a protection of sorts. Until recently, I've been able to live beneath the radar of ordinary society. I've been able to stay in proximity to you and your mother, to keep watch over you without fear of being recognized or taken seriously by anyone. I've had the freedom to pursue my objective: to find the fork and intercede.

And I suppose it goes beyond that too. The first two years here I lived in an apartment a few blocks from your house. It was hot in the winter and cold in the summer, with clever appliances and a TV set with an astonishing array of channels. And I came to despise it. I existed in the bleakest of conditions for too long a time to be properly civilized ever again. I could see how, if I let my guard down, I'd become as comfortable and selfish and corrupt as everybody else who made the journey. Sleeping under the stars at night reminds me where I come from and what needs to be done.

By making changes we open the future, but we lose our special knowledge and the power that goes with it. The leaders of your immigration aren't willing to give it up. They take advantage of this unnatural loophole. They hide here, making themselves comfortable for as long as possible.

They'll lose it all unless they keep this dying world intact. And they preach passivity in the name of caution. But it's nothing more than cowardice. Their knowledge, our knowledge, is dangerous and undeserved. Let's at least try to use it for good.

Your loving father,
Jonathan Santander (Poppy)

◆ ELEVEN

Ethan wants to go straight to the storage place in the Bronx and get to work, but I need to stop at home first.

'Just for a few minutes,' I tell him. 'Just to shower off and get clothes. I can't go around like this. And I have to talk to my mother before we disappear. I can't do that to her.'

'I think it's a bad idea.'

'I won't stay long enough for them to find me. Really. Hopefully, they're roaming around the squash courts in Spring Valley.'

The most pressing thing for me is my mom. I feel desperate to tell her what happened to Poppy and what I've learned. I can't go on without her knowing. And the pills. I have to tell her about them.

Ethan finally agrees to wait around the corner for me. I promise to be back in ten minutes or less. He hugs me. I feel his lips briefly graze the top of my ear.

'I'll see you in a minute,' I say.

'Right.'

'It's okay.' I say it to myself. It's hard to let go of him.

The house is mostly dark when I let myself in. I'm afraid my mom won't be there, but she is. I can't see her face well, but I see the worry in her posture as she walks toward me the moment I open the door.

'Prenna!' Her voice is a shriek. Even in the darkness she takes in the stains on my clothes. 'Are you all right? What is going on?'

I throw myself at her. It's a strange thing for me to do. But she doesn't retreat. She puts her arms around me. I'm worried she's been crying.

'Molly, he's been here the whole time,' I say with a sob. 'Poppy has been here. He came later than us, so he was old, but he arrived at the same place. Tonight somebody killed him. I was there. I held him when he died.'

I am sorry to put her through the same one-two I suffered: Poppy's alive and Poppy's dead.

She's still holding me, but her body is stiff. She's

crying too. 'That's impossible.'

'There are so many things I have to tell you,' I rush on. I should be more careful – I know that on some level – but I can't make myself be. 'We have no idea what's going on, you know. The pills don't protect us. They are making us blind. The pills that you—'

'That's not true!' My mother sounds desperate. 'Who told you that? Did this man who said he was Poppy tell you that? Because Poppy did not come. No one came besides us.' She lets go of me. 'Please don't talk that way. Please don't say anything else.'

'But I have to. I don't have much time. I have to clean myself up and I have to go, and I have so many things to tell you.' Her words are a jumble and so are mine. 'I'll be away for a few days, and I'll be out of contact, but I'll be back, so don't worry. Poppy says this is the critical—'

'Prenna, stop.' She is terrified. 'You put your trust in the wrong people! Please be quiet.'

Suddenly I understand the tone of her voice. I hear more than see the presence of two men in the dining room. Ethan was right. I am stupid.

I glance at my mother. I calculate the distance to the door.

'Prenna, we need you to come with us,' Mr. Robert

says as he walks toward us. The other man moves to stand in front of the door.

I recognize from his size that the second man is Mr. Douglas, one of the other counselors. He's well over six feet tall and weighs at least twice as much as me. There's something in his hand I suspect is a gag.

I look at my mother. 'Don't let them.' I don't know why I say this. I am out of my mind. I know she can't help me.

'Please cooperate, sweetheart.' Her voice is begging. 'They won't let any harm come to you if you cooperate. They've promised me that.'

'Don't let them take me.' My voice is rising. 'Don't trust them.'

'Prenna, be calm,' Mr. Robert orders. I know how much he wants to avoid a struggle. He hates anything ugly or unpleasant.

I consider for a moment the neighbors. I glance at Mr. Douglas and feel a tinge of fear. I don't think he has the same compunction as Mr. Robert.

I look around, frantic. 'I need to shower and get my things.'

'We have what you need for now. Your mother can collect more of your things later,' Mr. Robert says.

'But look at me.'

'There's a shower where we're going.' Mr. Robert has my arm and is aiming me toward the door. 'Let's not make it difficult,' he says.

He's sweating and breathing heavily, and I really loathe him.

'We'll call you in the morning, Molly, and let you know the next steps,' Mr. Robert says to my sobbing mother as we cross the hallway.

I sit in the back of Mr. Douglas's car, my arms wrapped around my body. It won't take Ethan long to figure out what happened. I am ashamed.

Will he try to follow? Mr. Douglas keeps looking up at the rearview mirror, as though he's expecting just such a contingency. What if they lead Ethan somewhere secret and remote and make him as vulnerable to them as I am? What would they do to him? The counselors are happy to tyrannize us travelers in any way they like, but would they touch a native? It would break so many rules.

And then I wonder, do the counselors take the rules seriously? What about the leaders? Do they really believe in them? Do they stick to them if it means sacrificing their own desires? Or are the rules just for keeping us in line?

As we wind through one neighborhood after the next, I have a sickening thought. *They took Katherine but they left me.* Maybe they let me go free only long enough to lead them to the old man. I am to blame for what happened to him, and now that he's gone my use to them is over.

They'll kill her if they have to. He knew what they were capable of. Did they kill him? *I am so sorry, Poppy,* I say to him in my thoughts.

I lie down, resting my warm cheek on the leather seat. I tuck my knees into my chest, like a fetus. Mr. Douglas is making turn after turn, and the car is silent. I should try to keep track of where we're going, but I can't.

My heart aches to think of Ethan carrying me to the car, holding me with both arms, stroking my hair. There's an ache and there's a longing. The separation feels like a physical pain.

What if, after everything, that is all we get? After years of tying myself in knots to keep the truth of who I am from Ethan, it turns out he knew from the moment I got here – before I even knew. The sweatshirt, my forbidden touchstone, folded up and hidden away all the time in the highest part of my closet. That was him too.

I think of the old man's flickering eyes, Poppy's eyes, that last moment of recognition.

I wish I had some happiness I could keep.

I feel tears trickling over the bridge of my nose and landing in my hair. I go back to one of my last memories before we made the trip here. I despaired over saying goodbye to Tiny, my grandmother, and my friend Sophia. 'Why are we leaving them?' I remember asking my mother.

She said it was because we needed to fix a few things, to make the world better for the people we loved. I believed it, and back then even she believed it.

But it was never going to happen, was it? We are just parasites. We haven't fixed anything. We haven't helped anybody but ourselves, and we left the rest to die.

And the secrets? All the spying. All the rules. They are for our protection. That's all they are for.

These days will pass, and I'll be in an attic or a basement or a cell somewhere, or maybe buried in the ground. May 17 will come and will go, and the world will keep on spinning toward its ruin.

I feel everything hopeful and good draining out of me like blood out of my veins. I imagine I am my father lying in the parking lot of an A&P with his throat open, his life leaking out, and nothing warm left.

◆

We end up someplace far away. Some kind of farm. Not in a happy way with animals or anything. Just a few buildings surrounded by fields and some giant spreading trees casting malevolent shadows. Mr. Douglas seems to know his way around. The place they put me is the basement of a small house – a guesthouse, maybe – a few yards away from the big house. It smells like new paint and new carpet. There's a room with a bed and a dresser and a desk, and a small bathroom and that's it. There are two small, high windows.

'I've left basic toiletries, a change of clothes, your *second* pair of glasses, and your vitamins in the bathroom. I'll pick up more of your things from your mother tomorrow. Get ready for bed quickly and turn out the lights. There's an intercom connecting to the main house if you need something.'

I sit on the bed.

'And, Prenna? You need to take the pills. You think you know what they are for, but you have no idea.'

I bow my head. There's no point in arguing.

'On Sunday morning we'll take you to a comfortable place upstate, where you'll be secure and can stay longer term.' He starts out the door.

'You mean like a terrific boarding school?'

He turns around. 'No. I told you. Katherine isn't being

punished. That's not the case for you.'

I hate him. 'How comfortable?' I demand. 'As comfortable as the place you sent Aaron Green?'

He hates me too. I can see it in his face. 'That will depend on you,' he says.

I don't take my vitamins. I don't care what they say. For the first time since we came here, I skip the little yellow pill. Or rather, I flush it down the toilet. I put my glasses on for now. Are the rules like the vitamins? Whom do they protect and whom do they hurt?

I can see a small piece of the moon from the high window over the desk. The window doesn't appear to open. I wonder how difficult it would be to break it. Probably pretty difficult. Could I fit through it if I did? Hard to say. It's like pulling up at a parking space – it's hard to know how big you are. And then I wonder how fast the counselors would appear if they heard breaking glass over the intercom. Or if I tried to disable the intercom. Even besides the intercom and my glasses, there's probably a camera and a microphone set up somewhere in the room.

I don't even care about where they are sending me on Sunday. I don't care what happens there. I'm not scared of that. I'm scared of Sunday, because it's May 18.

Because it is one day too late.

I shower, I change my clothes, I don't sleep. I think about Ethan. Where is he now? Did he see them taking me from my house?

At seven in the morning Mr. Robert opens my door and presents a plate of eggs and toast. He's already wearing a tie. Plain navy blue today. I put the plate on the desk. I won't eat it. I won't sleep and I won't eat. There's no living to be done here.

I want to ask him about the 'vitamins' and the glasses and the plans he promised all this time for averting the catastrophe. I want to ask him what really happened to my father and what it's like to tell lies all day long. I also want to punch him in the face.

I just sit there.

'Try not to look so stupid, Prenna,' he says.

Today is Thursday. I am losing hope. Saturday is the day. I stand on the desk and press my face to the high window. From the point of view of a bug in the grass I see a field, some trees, a dirt driveway. What am I going to do?

I watch the driveway. In the late morning a car drives along it and turns onto the road and fades into the distance. It's the only car sound I've heard. From the shape in the driver's seat I think it's Mr. Douglas.

One thing gives me a small feeling of possibility. I take my glasses off, and I keep looking out the window. I am still a bug in the grass, but every hour that passes, I see a little farther.

 TWELVE

That night I stand on the desk, watching through the window for the moon. The sky is a dull, dark clouded blue. What if I never see the moon? I try to fight off the feeling of despair.

Suddenly I startle at the glimpse of a pale face looking down. It isn't the moon. The face bends closer. It is the pinkish pale face of Ethan. He puts his fingers against the glass, five round white dots. I press my fingers to his. I want to cry. I want to get out of here so bad.

He waves me away from the window and I understand. We can't draw attention. I sit on the bed. I am not breathing at all. I can barely make out what he's doing in the nearly complete darkness, but I can faintly hear the glass-cutting knife scoring the edges of the window.

I need to do something to cover the sound, faint

though it is. They won't buy singing or talking to myself. So I do what I've done before in this room. I cry. I snuffle, I sob. It comes naturally. I imagine Mr. Robert backing away from the intercom. He is uncomfortable with emotion. He is uncomfortable with what they are doing to me.

Slowly, carefully, Ethan notches the glass and pops it out in one piece. I go into the bathroom. I turn the shower on full blast and then close the door, hoping the light and noise in the bathroom will blot out other activity. I creep across the room and climb up onto the desk. Ethan reaches his hand through and I take it. It's probably good I haven't eaten in two days.

He lays his jacket along the bottom to cover the sharp edge. He takes my other hand and pulls me up until most of my body is on the grass. Still, I try not to breathe. I climb out the rest of the way.

Quietly elated and terrified, I follow him across the lawn. I see the woods just a few dozen yards ahead. Without stopping, I take off my glasses and crack them into pieces, dropping them on the grass. I should have left them behind in the room, but there's no going back now. We don't slow down until we are deep into the woods, at least a mile from the farm.

Ethan loosens his grip on my hand, and we walk for

another couple of miles. At last we cross a road. We keep walking until we reach a gas station. My legs are scratched and aching, and I am exultant.

'This is right near where I parked,' he says. He goes into the store and gets two bottles of water and some candy bars. I follow him down the road to a car, a newish-looking Honda Accord, not his.

'I swapped with a neighbor,' he explains. 'Makes us harder to trace if it comes to that.'

I nod. I wait until we are safely in the car to ask. 'How did you find me?'

He turns the key in the ignition. 'I stuck a tracker into the sole of your sneaker after they took Katherine away.'

My eyes open wide.

'I know. I'm sorry. It's something they would do,' he says.

I heave a long breath. I gaze at him, on the verge of tears. 'Do you know how grateful I am?' He hands me a Snickers bar and I unwrap it blissfully. 'Maybe you need to think like them to beat them,' I say.

'I first came late last night to look around,' he says. 'I figured out where you were and what I needed, and I came back.'

'You are smarter than they are.'

'They are not as careful as I expected,' he says.

'Because they can't imagine anyone would actually go outside the community and rely on a time native for help.'

'Time natives?'

I never imagined I'd be saying that term to an actual time native and that it might sound patronizing when I did. 'People like you, who belong here. People other than us,' I say. For the first time in four years I'm not thinking in lies. I am not composing any or protecting any. I'm just talking.

'That's why you could never talk to me.'

'Yes. They don't trust time natives, none of us do, and we are forbidden to make close connections to them or tell them anything about ourselves. They keep us isolated and afraid. And they know that nobody from inside the community is going to help me. That makes them a little complacent, you could say.'

Ethan gives me a look. '*None* of you trust them?'

I shrug and smile at him. 'One of us seems to, no matter how much trouble it brings.'

Ethan takes a moment to pull me toward him. In exhaustion and relief he presses his face into my neck, and I wish I could stay there. I breathe him in, but only for a moment. 'There are other problems too,' I say warily, pulling away.

'What do you mean?'

'It's not a good idea for me to be too close to you or to . . .'

'What?'

'To be physically . . . intimate.' I am suddenly embarrassed. 'Not that that's what you were thinking or anything.' Sitting in this proximity, knowing the feeling of his arms, I am ashamed of the lustful thoughts I had about him when it was all just pretend.

He looks concerned and a little bit rueful. 'No. Right.' I can't tell if he's teasing me. 'But why do you say that? Nobody's watching us. You're past the point of obeying. You're a scofflaw through and through.' He stops himself and smiles. He meets my eyes. 'Not that I was planning to take advantage or anything.'

I nod slowly. 'It's not just that, though.' I try to think of how to say it. 'Because of where I come from, it can be dangerous.'

'How?'

'Well, certain changes happen in our cells and our immune systems over time. We were exposed to different strains of microbes – you know, viruses and bacteria and all that – than you were. We have different immunities. That's one of the reasons they won't let us near any medical treatment here. They say if a lab gets a look at our blood, it could raise all kinds of impossible questions.

Our scientists had the advantage of knowing the disease landscape from the past – I mean, from now – so they could give us shots to protect us. They still give us shots twice a year. And the pills we take are part of that – or at least, they are supposed to be.'

He looks relieved. 'So you're safe.'

'Yes. But you're not.'

'I'm not?'

'You're not safe from me. You don't have immunities to the germs I carry. I come from a place with illnesses you can't even imagine. Blood plagues that destroyed our families. I am immune to the plague – we all are who came here, because otherwise we'd be dead. But who knows what little shifts there have been in my RNA or whatever that I could pass on to you.'

'Just by being close to me? I don't believe that.'

'The leaders seem to think very casual contact is safe enough. What they warn us about is anything deeper than that. That's one of the reasons why the rule about intimacy with time natives is so strict. They say it could be like Cortés arriving among the Aztecs and wiping them all out with European smallpox.' I feel myself deflating as I say it. It's not a very romantic thing to have to tell the only boy you ever thought you loved.

He looks at me carefully. He is quiet for a while and

132

then he shakes his head. 'I'm not scared of that. I'm not scared of you.'

I take a deep breath. 'I am.'

The mood as we drive is sober. As we cross from New York State into New Jersey, Ethan reaches out for my hand. I can sense in his face the look of dawning rebellion.

We eventually end up parked at a rest stop off the Palisades. The storage place doesn't open until seven, and we need to try to sleep. We've got a couple of big days ahead.

'Where do your parents think you are?' I ask him, imagining for a moment a more ordinary life.

'Visiting my sister at Bucknell for a long weekend.'

'And what does your sister think?'

'She thinks I've got a secret girl.'

He gets a blanket out of the trunk and opens the door for me. 'You lie down in the back and try to sleep, okay?' He hands me the blanket.

'What about you?'

He gets back into the driver's seat. 'I'm really good at sleeping sitting up.'

'You sure?'

'Yeah, and that way, I can get us out of here quickly if we need to.'

'Do you think they are going to find us?'

'I think they are going to try, but I think we have the advantage. Kenobi said they are good at oppressing their captives, but they have no traction in the real world. I can navigate it a lot better than they can.'

'You think?'

'Sure. They have no real contacts among the time natives, as you say.'

'Not really, no.'

'And you, my friend – you definitely do.'

He locks the doors, and the car is dark and quiet. I see the condensation from our breath on the windows. I hear the cars zooming by on the Palisades Parkway. I have no reason to feel safe, but I do.

I'm so close to Ethan, it's hard to sleep. I hear him shifting and turning in the front seat. I listen to him breathe.

After a long time of quiet nonsleeping I hear him get out of the front seat and open the door to the back. My heart lifts when he climbs in, though I know it shouldn't. I sit up to make room.

'No, no, lie down,' he says. 'Is there room for me?'

I squeeze over. He lies down next to me. I spread the blanket over the two of us.

'I'm not really very good at sleeping sitting up.'

I laugh.

At first we lie like two sardines, back to back on the narrow seat. But soon Ethan turns over and I feel his arms come around me. I feel his heart beating against my back. 'This is casual, right?' he says.

'I don't think it's what they meant,' I say. He's been this close before with no ill effects so far. 'But I think it's okay.'

As I get drowsy his legs entwine with mine.

'Hey, Prenna?' I feel him whispering into my neck.

'Yeah?'

'If it was okay for me to kiss you,' he whispers, 'would you want me to?'

I know I should lie. I should make this easier on both of us. But I've begun to tell the truth, and I am drunk on it. 'The most of anything,' I whisper into the seat.

'Me too.' I feel him kiss my shoulder blade before he lays his head down and goes to sleep.

 # THIRTEEN

We park in a lot in the Bronx and study the street map on his phone. Or he studies it. My eyes aren't that good yet. We take a wrong turn before we get our bearings. The streets are run-down and deserted. Most buildings look uninhabited, judging from the broken windows. I don't really fear the threats they've got here in this part of the twenty-first century, but still I am grateful not to be alone.

It's a cold morning and the wind is blowing Ethan's T-shirt. He looks filthy and banged up from two nights creeping around a farm. And tired. But he's jumping around on the sidewalk like a lunatic.

'What are you doing?'

'It's just, I don't know. I feel so healthy. Energetic.' He's a little winded, but smiling broadly.

I watch him jump a few more times. 'Oh, you do, do you?' I think I know what he's getting at.

'Not sick at all in any way.'

I stare at him suspiciously.

He shrugs. 'Just saying.'

We find the address, a big square industrial building with a giant well-lit billboard on the roof advertising to cars whooshing by on the elevated expressway above us.

At the desk is a bored-looking attendant with a laminated ID card hanging around his neck. His name is Miguel. He takes his headphones off.

'Card?' he says.

I hand it to him.

'Can I see your key?'

I hand him that too.

'Compartment number?'

I pause. I really don't want to raise his suspicions. It's enough that we're filthy and groggy-looking teenagers showing up at seven in the morning. 'Five one seven.' I try not to say it as a question.

He checks his computer and pushes the digital pad toward me. 'Sign here, please.'

I sign illegibly, which is not worse than I usually sign on those things.

'Elevator to five, two rights and a left,' he says. He

leans back in his chair and puts his headphones back on.

It's an elevator big enough to drive a car into. I swipe the card to open the fifth floor so the button lights up. My hands are sweating and I can't keep my feet still.

'We shouldn't spend more time here than we have to,' Ethan says as we stride along the concrete hallway. I know it's on both our minds that we might not be the only ones who know about this place.

I nod. There are a few thickly paned windows, through which the rushing lights of the cars on the expressway give a sickening strobelike effect.

I am squinting, trying to keep my hand steady as I turn the key in the lock. The knob turns and I push the door open. I zip the key into my jacket pocket.

Ethan feels along the wall for the light switch and turns on an overhead fluorescent light that sputters and blinks before it comes on.

It's a room about six feet wide and nine feet deep. There are rough plywood shelves covering two walls, and they are almost entirely empty. Along one middle shelf on one wall there are four file boxes and a red binder.

I step in and Ethan follows. He takes a look behind him at the door. 'Leave it open?'

It would make me claustrophobic to close it. The

hallway is deserted. 'Yeah.'

'Start here?' he asks, picking up the first box.

I nod. I'm working my courage up to touch anything.

'It's a bunch of newspapers,' he says, and I wonder if I hear a trace of disappointment in his voice. Maybe he was hoping for some mind-blowing technology.

'Not very futuristic,' I say.

'No. Do you mind if I look?'

'Go ahead.'

I put my fingers around the second box. I cajole myself a little to open it. It's not just the fear of knowledge, but years of being brainwashed never to invade privacy or look where you aren't supposed to look. Some emotions, like safety and trust, are tough for us to come by, and others, like guilt and suspicion, are right on tap all the time.

The box is divided into several compartments, and one of them has my initials – my old initials – written in black marker. In the spirit of Ellis Island immigrants, none of us kept our old last names when we moved here.

The first thing is a dry piece of paper with a crayon drawing of a family made crudely and childishly with stick legs and oval feet, large round-fingered hands and lollipop heads. There is a father with straight black hair and a beard, a mother with yellow hair holding an egg-shaped baby in blue, a big girl with dark hair like her father and gray-blue spots for eyes like her mother. She is holding hands with – or overlapping hands with – a little dark-haired boy.

It takes a strange act of relaxation to connect this drawing to myself. To connect the memory of drawing it, which I do faintly have, to my hands, my eyes, my thoughts. I try to connect the little girl in that memory to the person I am now.

Under it is a birthday card for my father, also made by the little girl in my memory – that being me. And another and another, the first one barely a scribble, and my name printed with oversized, uppercase letters, half of them backwards, with shoes at the bottoms, as though I'd never written letters before. Me. My name. Writing a card to my father.

I sit on the floor and pull the box into my lap. There are my earliest efforts at forming the alphabet and the numbers up to twenty, spelling tests administered by my dad, half a page describing my new baby brother, my first book report, on *Misty of Chincoteague*.

There are essays I wrote on the creation of the Internet, the water crisis of 2044, the great blizzard of '72, which dumped over four feet of snow along the Eastern Seaboard in a single night. I remember them more than read them. There is a grade at the top of each one. I begged my dad to give me grades so I could feel like the real students I read about in books, and not just a kid writing papers in her kitchen.

There is the essay I began on the blood plague of '87 but didn't finish. The date under my name is 2095. I remember the excuse I made for abandoning it and also the true reason. The plague was coming back. It wasn't history; it was hovering and buzzing outside our door. It was better to write essays about things that had ended, I decided, and it was starting to seem like the blood plagues had only just begun.

Another section of the box has a lot of my mother's stuff: folded college and medical school diplomas, various certificates and awards. It is touching to me that my father saved it all. Her lab closed down in the late seventies, so there's not much after that. I find a clipping from her college paper, and I wish I could see it better. I can only read the big type declaring her the winner of the intercollegiate debate competition. A debater! I find that pretty impossible to imagine. I look at the picture of her broad, confident smile. *Are you really my mother?* I want to ask that girl in the picture.

I can't look anymore. The memories in the box connect me more and more to the memories inside of me, each one tying me to my old self like another length of string. Each one is reminding me of my Poppy, who is slowly, painfully edging toward the old man dying in my lap.

This is the past I was ordered to forget. It is here; it happened. It is part of me, what made me who I am.

Just because it hasn't happened yet doesn't mean it hasn't happened. It has. It is real. I am real. I am not some fabrication, out of nothing and nowhere, floating through time. I had a real family. I belonged somewhere once.

I hear the crumpling of paper behind me and I turn around. I bring myself back to this time, this room, this Ethan.

'What do you see?' I ask.

'This newspaper is from Tuesday.'

I stand up and go over to him.

'Not last Tuesday, but Tuesday coming up.'

It is indeed a curled and yellowed edition of the *New York Times*, reporting on a day that hasn't happened yet. I squint at the date. I know this particular Sunday. I've thought a lot about this Sunday. Because it is the day too late.

'What about the other ones?' I see there's a stack of

them he's piled neatly on the floor.

He hands the Sunday one to me. 'This was on top. It's the one he obviously spent the most time on. It looks like it's been pulled apart and read a lot, which makes sense.'

I nod. I fold it and put it in the duffel bag Ethan brought in case we need to make a quick exit.

'There's maybe ten or so papers altogether. One from 2010 and each of the years up until now.' He shakes his head, and his eyes look slightly out of focus. 'I didn't realize they would *keep going*. Look.' He pulls out another pile from the shelf and carefully flips through them. 'Two more from this month, another from late this year, one from next year, another from the year after that, and then . . .' He examines the last paper in the box. 'Unbelievable. June 2021.'

'That's a late one,' I say, a little dizzy.

'How long did they go?'

I try to remember my history lessons. 'I don't think there was any news printed on paper after the early twenties,' I say.

'Unbelievable,' he says again. 'So they went purely digital after that?'

'Basically, yes. But the whole delivery of news had changed out of the newspaper format by then.'

'That's why I am surprised to see all this paper,' Ethan says. 'I mean, even right now newspaper is kind of antique. I'd figured he'd have everything saved on some insane kind of drive or memory device. How much easier it would be to transport and preserve it than paper . . .'

I am not so surprised. My father loved paper, even from before. 'Think about it,' I say. 'A paper is an object. An actual thing. It can't be modified, overwritten, updated, refreshed, hacked or anything else. It is fragile, but it's a snapshot of history that hasn't been messed with. It's one version of history we know happened.'

Ethan nods. 'I see what you mean.'

'For now people are thrilled about everything digital, endless data farms, your own piece of the cloud and all that. Nobody has much respect for paper at the moment, but I think the excitement kind of dies down after a while,' I tell him. 'As time goes on I think people, definitely my father, come back around to respect the power of actual things you can actually touch.'

Ethan picks up next Sunday's paper. 'I'm almost scared to look at this. Do you know what it means?'

'I think so.' I hear the rush of cars outside and feel a chill.

'Do you know how much power this one piece of paper could give you?'

'I do. Especially if it's accurate.'

'Why wouldn't it be? You just said it was a snapshot of history.'

'It is. But it's one snapshot of one history.'

Ethan's face is uneasy. He knows where I'm going.

'There's a thing this paper shows us that's more important than the stock quotes and the sports scores and the history of the day it was printed,' I say.

'What's that?'

'How much we've changed things. Now that we're here from the future, messing around, if a gap opens up between what's happening in the world and what this newspaper says, we can see the impact we've made since it was printed.'

'What do you make of this?' Ethan hands me the red folder.

Inside the folder is a pile of loose sheets, each with a photo of a person; some printed information, mostly medical records; and a bunch of handwritten notes. On the top is a woman named Theresa Hunt. She was born in 1981. I'm having trouble reading the smaller print, but my eyes dart down to a note circled in red pen: *Patient #1?*

The second is a boy, aged three, named Jason Hunt.

I'm guessing he's Theresa's son. *Patient #2?* says the note.

There are at least a dozen other sheets with similar kinds of information. They aren't all numbered as patients, but each is clearly related to the same project. Are these people sick? Are they still alive? 'I think he could be trying to create an early medical history of the plague. I'm not sure.' I flip to the last sheet of paper. 'I didn't think the blood plague got started quite this early, but it's possible, I guess. Maybe there was some kind of precursor to it.' I know the disease mutated a bunch of times, getting worse with each one. In the beginning it was harder to transmit and by the end it was carried by mosquitoes. I'm not ready to get too deep into this with Ethan yet.

I put the folder in the duffel bag to study when we have more time and my eyes are working better.

I move on to the third of the file boxes. I open it and let out a breath.

'What?' Ethan asks.

'There's money in here. Piles of cash. Mostly hundreds and fifties. I hope he wasn't robbing banks.'

'I doubt he was.'

I check all the sections of the box and they contain the same. 'God, there's a lot.' I examine the dates on the money. Some of it is from 2008, 2009, up to the present.

146

In another envelope the dates on the bills are from next year and the year after that. 'He must have brought it back with him.'

'I wonder how he collected all that. It looks like a lot. Was he rich?'

I try to remember what I learned. 'It's not that. There was crazy inflation of US dollars in the fifties, I think. I remember my dad told me it cost two hundred and fifty dollars to ride the subway in 2056 and five hundred dollars to buy a doughnut.'

'You're kidding me. How much did it cost when you were a kid?'

'I can't really say. The US gave up on the dollar and made a new currency by the early sixties, and another one by the late sixties. Goldbacks was the name of the money we used when I was little. None of it kept its value, and anyway, by then you couldn't buy a doughnut at any price. The old green dollars were mostly destroyed, I guess. But I remember seeing them around once in a while. I even remember burning them in the fireplace. They were useless otherwise.'

Ethan is looking a little shell-shocked. 'They are pretty useful around here.'

'I know. That surprised me when we came here. It's hard to have any respect for these pieces of paper we used to chuck into the fireplace.'

'Your father must have salvaged these, knowing they would come in handy.'

'You see what I mean about his devotion to paper?' I hand one of the piles to Ethan so he can see for himself.

He calculates. 'There's got to be a hundred thousand dollars in that box.'

'I'll put some in our bag to bring with us,' I say.

'Make sure you pick a stack of bills that have already been printed.'

I check the dates of the first stack and put it in our bag. 'Never know when you might need' – I quickly try to calculate the clump of bills – 'five thousand dollars.'

He opens his eyes wide. 'What are you going to do with the rest of it?'

'Leave it for now, I guess. We've got more important stuff to think about.'

I turn to the last box. I see thin, semitransparent black cards arranged in decks. They are instantly familiar to me and yet I haven't seen them since we left. 'You'll like these better,' I say to Ethan.

He comes over to examine them.

'These are memory banks, one card for each month. Each deck is a year.' I pull one out. 'I'm not sure what device could read them here. But if you could find one, you would see the future.'

'What do you mean by "memory banks"?'

'It starts soon, like in the next three years, if I'm remembering my history lessons right,' I tell him. 'People start banking their memories. It's very simple. You have the technology right now – everyone does who has a phone, basically. It's the same principle the counselors use for our glasses. If you hold up your phone and keep the movie camera on for every waking hour, you can record everything you do and everything you see and everything you hear. Which would be dumb and cumbersome and you wouldn't do it, but you get the idea.

'The first gizmo people adopted in a big way was called iMemory, this tiny microphone-camera combo about the size of a pearl you could wear as an earring, on a necklace or really any place. After a while they got even tinier and people started getting them implanted in their earlobes. It automatically records everything you see and do in the course of a day, and it all uploads and stores automatically to your own spot on the data cloud. Most of it you ignore, of course, because it is dead boring. But say you lost your wallet or your keys or your phone and need to figure out where you put them. Say you wanted to prove that you really did take out the garbage or finish your math homework or that your sister hit you first, or whatever. With memory banking you can go to the tape and it's easily searchable. You can search it by date, by hour, by keyword. You can retrace any part of your life you want.' I haven't thought about iMemory in a long time. 'Not that people do it much, but they like to know they *can*. In the beginning people used to say it was almost like being immortal, being able to hold on to your whole life like that.

'It may sound weird right now, but you'll all be doing it soon. It's great for some things – like the crime rate, for example. Nobody gets away with anything. The problem starts when other people besides you have access to your life.'

I hold up a deck. 'These are my dad's. This one's from 2058. That might be the earliest one. Here. This is 2086. That's the year I was born.'

He tugs on a strand of my hair. 'I could see you being born?'

'Yeah, maybe. If we get through this week.' I pull out decades of my father's memories and under them find decks with my mother's initials.

'Unbelievable,' Ethan says.

I pull them out, re-creating the years in order. My eyes are aching, but I strain to read the dates. I find my own memories. Four and a half decks of them. I didn't start banking until I was seven. And then I see there is one incomplete deck that comprises the brief life and memory of Julius. I put it all back, close the box and latch it. I put my hands over my face. What would I see if I looked through his eyes?

I stand. That's all I can take for now.

Ethan is studying a yellowed piece of paper he found among the memory banks in the last box. Something about his posture alarms me.

'Ethan?'

No answer. I walk over to him. He is staring at a deeply faded drawing. I strain my eyes to make out the pencil marks. 'That looks old,' I say. 'What is it?'

Still no answer. I bend closer to see it. It's a sketch of a storm of some kind. It's got some arrows and diagrams to one side. Across the bottom is a map.

'Are you okay?' I ask.

Ethan looks up from the drawing. I have never seen him like this before. 'Do you know what this is?' he asks.

'No.'

'It's mine. It's a drawing I made of the day at the river I described to you. The day you came through and I found you.'

'Did you give it to him?'

'No. That's what I don't understand, Pren. It is sitting in the bottom drawer of my desk in my room.'

'Right now?'

'Right now.'

'Are you sure?'

'I am absolutely sure.'

'Did you make a copy?'

'There is no copy.'

I consider this. 'So you mean you haven't given it to him yet.'

January 2012
Dear Julius,

Mom caught me writing this letter to you. She says I can't write to you ever again or she'll tell Mr. Robert. I told her I write in the dark and no one knows, but she still said no.

So this is my last one for now, and I just want to say that this place we live in now is beautiful. It's hard being here in a lot of ways, but yesterday I walked home from school through the park and snow was falling, and I felt like the luckiest person in the world.

The hardest part is not having you here with me, but it's not nearly as hard as it used to be. It used to be that your life had ended, but now that we're here, it hasn't even begun. We are fixing things, so when your life does begin you are going to get to do the greatest stuff. You're going to swim in the ocean and eat mangoes anytime you want. And you're going to see squirrels and carpenter bees and maybe have a dog for a pet. And I'm going to show you how to plant these oniony bulbs that become flowers in the spring.

It's going to be a better life for us, J. You are going to get to grow up this time, I promise you.

Love,

Your sister, Prenna

♦ FOURTEEN

It is still early Friday. We are driving along the Meadowbrook Parkway as though in a dream. The sun is shining and I've got one bare foot out the window, feeling the wind through my toes.

We stop at Target to buy a prepaid phone.

'Go ahead, splurge,' Ethan says to me jokingly when I hold up two. I guess it's not every day we come upon thousands of dollars.

I use one of the phones to call my mother. I've been wondering what she knows, whether they told her I got away. I know how they hate to admit mistakes or ever let on that they are not in control.

'Molly, I can only talk for a second,' I tell her breathlessly when she picks up. I have a lurking fear they will somehow trace the call if I stay on too long.

'Prenna! Where are you?'

'I'm fine. I got away from Mr. Robert, and no one is hurt. I need to try to fix something Poppy told me about, but I'll be home by Sunday at the latest.' I hear voices in the background. I realize she's not alone. 'Mom?'

'Prenna?' Now it's a different voice. I think it's Ms. Cynthia on the phone. It's a voice that curdles my blood. 'Can you hear me, Prenna? You'll make life very unpleasant for your mother if you persist in this. And for Katherine.'

She is grotesque. I should hang up. 'They didn't do anything.'

'All the more reason you should bear them in mind.'

'I'm not the one wanting to hurt them!' It's the twelve-year-old me, rising to defend us against the insidious Ms. Cynthia. I need to calm down. She starts to talk but I talk over her. 'I'll be back in two days. You leave them alone, and I will go straight to Mr. Robert's door and turn myself in. You can do whatever you want to me then. But if you hurt them, I swear I will bring EVERYTHING down.' I hang up. I crack the phone in two at the joint and throw it across the parking lot.

I walk a few yards away from the car, crouch down and put my face in my hands. A minute or so later I feel Ethan's hand on my back.

'That didn't go so well.'

'Not so well.' I stand up. I wipe my eyes. 'It's going to be okay, though.'

'Yeah?'

'Yeah.' And somehow I know it's true, because for the first time in the history of Ms. Cynthia it wasn't me who sounded scared. It was her.

This may be the first hour of freedom I've had in my life here, so we decide we ought to go see the ocean in person. 'We've got to be somewhere,' Ethan says philosophically, and that does appear to be true.

My vision is really clearing, and it feels miraculous. It is different and better than it ever was through those piece-of-crap glasses. Driving along the shore under a blue sky and a washy yellow sun with the dunes of the Atlantic Ocean just beyond my window, the planet feels scrubbed new and so beautiful.

Ethan glances at me and smiles.

We drive out to Jones Beach, to Field Two, and park near the snack bar. It is already filling up. Why not? It's a beautiful and very warm Friday in May.

'This is perfect,' Ethan says as we watch clusters of people in beach gear stream by, dragging coolers and umbrellas and a few small children. 'What better place for a couple of folks running for their lives and concerned with the fate of humanity?'

For the moment, though, we stay in the car. Ethan takes out the *New York Times* from this coming Sunday and divides it into parts.

'You can properly read now, can't you?' Ethan asks, watching me trying out the small print on the front page, as proud as if he'd taught me himself.

We are playing it cool, but I can tell we are both uneasy, afraid to open the paper and look inside. When my family emigrated, we travelers brought so few artifacts back with us that this newspaper is almost as strange to me as it is to Ethan.

I start with the weather at the top. 'You could find success as a weather forecaster with these papers,' I say.

Ethan is glancing uncertainly at the sports section. 'And make a bloody fortune gambling on sports scores. I always start with this page, but it seems so wrong to look at it.'

'I know what you mean.' I take that and the business section and put them to the side. 'Let's not worry about these for now.'

Together, we page through the front section. Just glancing from headline to headline, column to column, I don't see anything that strikes me as out of step with the general stream of news, at least not so far as I follow it. The immigration has apparently done a good job of not fixing anything. Maybe it has also succeeded in preventing uncontainable changes.

At one point Ethan puts down the paper and just gazes at me like, *How did we get here?* My heart goes out to him. I am used to the world being out of order.

I think of the look on his face when he found his drawing in Poppy's storage box. He's been through a lot today and it's not even noon.

I touch my fingers to his wrist. 'I'm sorry to get you mixed up in all this.'

For a moment he looks at me in our old way. 'I'm already so mixed up over you, Henny. Since the first day I saw you. There's no getting out of it now.'

'I think we should look at the Metro section,' I say, after we split a corn dog, a bag of chips and a lemonade from the snack bar and get back in the car. I unfold it and put it in front of us. Under the fold there is a prominent article accompanied by a photo of a man and a photo of a woman.

Ethan leans in. 'Holy shit, do you know who this is?' He means the woman. I move aside so he can scan the columns. His finger stops on her name at the top of the article. 'Yeah, it's definitely her.'

'Who?'

'Mona Ghali. The scientist who wrote the papers I told you about. At the lab where I interned last summer.'

'The paper you wanted to show to Ben Kenobi.'

'Exactly.'

'My God. What happened to her?'

We're both so agitated and flustered, we are reading all spasmodically and out of sequence. I go back to the headline. 'I think she's dead.' I read aloud, '*Lovers' Quarrel Turns Deadly.*' I try to slow down and read the first couple of paragraphs carefully and in order. 'I guess it turned deadly for her.' I point to the man. 'This guy' – I look for the name – 'Andrew Baltos killed her.'

Ethan looks aghast. He's stopped reading. 'She's dead?'

I check the date again, just to be sure. 'No. She's alive at the moment. She'll be dead on Saturday night at around seven-forty-five.'

Ethan is staring at the article without quite bringing himself to read it. 'Why? Why would anyone do that to her?'

'It seems to say this guy Andrew is her boyfriend and they had a fight.' I read on a little ways. 'The guy is not denying he killed her. He claims he did it in self-defense and that she had a gun.'

Ethan takes a moment to absorb this. 'Do you think this could be it?'

We both know what 'it' is. It's too momentous a coincidence not to be. 'I think so.' My hands flutter nervously as I refold the paper to get the crease out of the middle of the picture. 'Did my father know about her?'

'I told him about her work. Not the wave-energy work as much as the dark-matter stuff she was doing on the side. I don't know if I said her name. I never got the chance to give him that paper she wrote.'

I rest my eyes for a minute before I read on. 'And it was her birthday.'

'She got killed on her birthday? Gets killed?'

'Like Shakespeare. Shakespeare died on his birthday.' I finish the article. 'I thought we'd be looking for something like a political assassination or maybe even a corporate assassination. You know what I mean? I wasn't imagining a girl on her birthday in a fight with her boyfriend.'

Ethan is staring at the picture. 'Well, but this girl is kind of a special case.'

I go back to the paper. 'The lab is in Teaneck?'

'Yeah.'

'That's where it happened. Happens.'

He is shaking his head. 'Crazy. I've been there

probably a hundred times.'

'That could be useful, right?' I lay the newspaper on the dashboard to study the man's picture up close in full sunshine. 'We have to find out who this guy is. We should find out everything we can about him.'

Ethan is nodding. 'I've still got her paper in my backpack. I can't believe she's dead.'

'She's not.'

'Supposed to die, I mean.'

'We're going to keep her alive, remember?'

We scour the rest of the newspaper from May 18, just to be sure, and then read through the other three papers we brought, which take us through the end of the month.

We find something important almost right away. In the paper dated May 21, an article buried deep in the Metro section describes an unusual turn in the case of Mona Ghali and Andrew Baltos. What appeared to be a lovers' quarrel and an accidental killing in self-defense has begun to appear more complicated. Two computers in Mona Ghali's office were wiped nearly clean and a file cabinet was emptied.

We also have a newspaper from May 28, reporting that Mona Ghali's apartment had been messed with too. Files had been taken from her home computer, and the place had been thoroughly searched the night she died. Is supposed to die.

A related story from the May 27 paper, which we do not have, is also mentioned here. As soon as the plot started to thicken, Baltos disappeared before the police could take him into custody, and they think he fled the country with a fake passport.

'That is lame,' Ethan points out as I read it to him.

'He sounds like quite a mysterious character,' I say, looking up from the paper. 'He's not a US citizen, they can't figure out his real name, and they have no idea how he got here. He must have gotten into this country illegally.'

'So maybe it is more the way you were imagining,' Ethan says when I finish reading everything I can find. 'Baltos wanted to kill her – wants to kill her – for her work and the work she'll do in the future, and that is also the reason we need to save her.'

'But this guy doesn't know the work she'll do in the future. He doesn't have the kind of knowledge we have. He can't possibly know this is the fork.'

Ethan is staring at the man's picture again. 'Are you sure?'

'Well, he can't be part of our immigration.'

'How do you know?' Ethan asks.

'Because he's in this newspaper. These were written and printed before we came.'

'Right, of course.' Ethan shakes his head as though to straighten out his thoughts.

'Still, you can cause the fork without knowing you're causing the fork, obviously,' I say. 'And he must have suspected she was onto something. Was he trying to steal her research? Use it for his own glory?'

Ethan considers this. 'Well, if he did, he didn't get very far with it. The future as Ben Kenobi described it is a climate fiasco. It doesn't sound like it benefits from any revolution of zero-emissions wave energy.'

'No. It doesn't. It didn't. No glory there.'

'Maybe he's a corporate spy, working for big oil. You know, some big greedy oil conglomerate trying to squelch a new technology that could put them out of business. You read about stuff like that sometimes. Or maybe you just see it in movies.'

I stare at my toenails, thinking. 'It's a good theory. Hard to prove.'

Ethan shrugs. 'Too bad we can't do Internet searches of the near future. I mean, hey, it's only a couple days away.'

I laugh. 'Yeah, what's with that? You can't even look up tomorrow. Who says the Internet is boundless?'

◆

We leave the newspapers in the car and strategize while we walk along the sand. We run in and out of the cold, thrilling surf and make big plans, 'big, smart plans,' as Ethan says.

But once we figure those out, we realize the ocean is more fun when you have a bathing suit.

I guess without really saying it, we have the feeling that though tomorrow is a momentous day – nothing less than a day to change the world – today is something pretty momentous too. It's a little piece of time we can steal before we have to face our lives again.

So at Ethan's urging we leave Long Island and drive through Brooklyn, then cross Staten Island, heading an hour and a half down the coast of New Jersey until we find a tall pink hotel right on a boardwalk fronting a wide, crowded ocean beach.

It isn't a beautiful hotel or anything. It is your standard beachside tower from the 1970s with a lot of stucco and balconies, but it feels weirdly perfect.

Checking in is a little awkward. Ethan strides to the counter full of purpose and comes back from it looking confused.

'There's only one room available. It's got a queen-sized bed and a pull-out couch or something like that. I'll take the couch. Do you mind sharing?' This is such unfamiliar territory, he hasn't quite figured out how to joke about it.

'No. That's fine.'

Our room is on the seventh floor and has a partial ocean view, which means if you go out to the tiny balcony and crane your neck pretty far to the right, you can see a tiny sliver of it. Mostly the view is of a parking lot and an IHOP, and it is beyond my best hopes.

In one day I went from total hopelessness in a basement prison to being here, on the edge of the ocean, the edge of a true accomplishment and the edge of a pancake house, for God's sake, with a person I think I might really love. It is strange and thrilling to know that nobody else is watching what I do, seeing what I see, listening to what I say. For once.

Before I get too high, I think of Katherine. I wish she could taste this.

Two of the walls of the room are white and two are aqua colored. The bedspread is a rubbery floral, and the couch looks certain to be uncomfortable, but the room is bright and clean. There is a rough straw mat under my feet that smells like the beach. I go into the bathroom to check it out. I am euphoric over the little soaps and shampoos.

Do you know what this is like for me? I feel like shouting.

I can see! I can say what I think! I can use one little shampoo and take the other one home! I can imagine the future opening up so that none of us knows what's going to happen anymore!

Ethan throws the duffel bag on the couch and unzips it. In the closet is a safe. I hear him fiddling with it, and then he puts the money and papers in. He comes back and hands me a bunch of fifties and twenties. He tells me the combination to remember.

'We need to get a change of clothes,' he announces. 'You stink.'

He takes in my look of horror.

'Penny, I'm kidding.' He laughs. 'You don't stink at all. Or hardly at all, anyway.'

I glance down at the sweatpants and tank top I wore to go to bed two nights ago. 'Your hygiene isn't that impressive either.' I try to rally. It was easier to be lighthearted when the most serious business between us was hangman.

'Come on. There are stores along the boardwalk.'

I consider. This could be uncomfortable. I don't know how to think about him. He can't be my boyfriend, but I can't pretend there's not a potent attraction. I can't look at his eyes or his mouth or his hands with any neutrality, but I can't lead him on either. I can't help but begin to notice certain ways he looks at me, especially when he doesn't know I'm looking.

'Okay,' I finally say. I wash my face and wish I could brush my teeth, and we strike out for the town.

I get some toiletries at a blindingly bright drugstore. Ethan tags along as I pick out a toothbrush, toothpaste and a pink plastic hairbrush. In a distant way I think the old thoughts: *Am I doing this right? Would a normal person buy this? Am I giving anything away?*

He knows! I shout at myself. *He's known from the very beginning!*

Ethan disappears down an aisle and I take the opportunity to buy a three-pack of cotton underwear and a razor to shave my legs. What a lark to think of shaving my legs at such a time, but I do. He meets me again at the counter, somewhat triumphantly holding a pair of bright orange flip-flops, a phone to replace the one I broke, and a pack of cards.

Our next stop is a boutique selling a million pairs of sunglasses and piles of cheap beachwear. I look around uncertainly. I can barely shop with myself, let alone with an eighteen-year-old boy.

Ethan breaks the ice by trying on an absurd fringed shirt with a huge sunburst on the back.

I laugh.

'No?' he says, acting surprised.

I pick out an orange sarong, a pair of denim shorts, a white tank top, a gray sweatshirt, a wide-brimmed straw hat and a bathing suit. We're loaded, right?

Ethan is trying on oversized white plastic sunglasses as I toss my pile on the counter.

'Done,' I say.

'Aren't you going to try anything on?' Ethan looks disappointed.

'I don't need to,' I say quickly.

Ethan picks up the sarong and stretches it out in puzzlement. 'What do you do with this thing?'

'You tie it around yourself.'

'Show me?'

I tie it around his hips as a skirt.

'I meant you,' he says.

The sun-beaten, fifty-something-year-old sales lady plucks the bathing suit from the pile. 'This is nonreturnable, hon. And the sizes run big. You ought to try it on.'

I look suspiciously at Ethan's pleased face. It's as though he and the saleslady are in cahoots. He shrugs innocently.

I grab the bathing suit and trudge toward the fitting room in the back.

What's the big deal? He'll see me in a bathing suit soon enough. But my cheeks are warm as I try to make the curtain cover the door without the big gaps on the sides. Why do dressing rooms always have such terrible-fitting curtains?

I shed my clothes hurriedly and pull on the stretchy bottoms. They've got the papery sticker over the crotch that makes a crinkling noise as I move around. The top is a halter held together by a brown tortoiseshell ring in the middle. Of course there is no mirror. I have to slump out to the long mirror between the two changing rooms.

Do I really need to see how it looks? I think of Ethan standing out there. Nah, it's fine.

'How's the *fit*?' calls the saleslady's loud voice from about a foot away.

'Uh. It's fine.'

'Well, don't hide in there!' she says boomingly. 'You can't even *see* yourself!'

I look down at my skin, which looks bluish and mottled. Lovely.

This is a laid-back beach town. People here probably go out to dinner in bikinis half the size of this one. They probably go to church in less clothing than I am wearing. They are used to letting everything show, inside and out, and I am used to hiding everything.

I walk out. I try not to slouch into a ball.

'Very nice!' the saleslady exclaims. Nightmarishly, she turns me around to look at me from every angle. 'You've got a gorgeous *figure*,' she shouts, which is a word that particularly makes me wince.

I look at Ethan like, *Would you get a load of this person?* but his face has more color than usual too.

We leave the store with a full bag, including the fringed shirt and the oversized white sunglasses.

Ethan is jubilant, and I can't help smiling as we bounce along. 'That was by far the best time I've ever had shopping,' he says.

We find a place to eat burgers and milk shakes right on the beach. After we finish, Ethan and I drift down to the water and kick off our shoes. I pull my sweatpants up to my knees, he rolls up his pants and we wade into the water.

It is gentle and transparent, and the sunlight stabs right through. I dig my toes into the fine wet sand, trying to think of nothing other than the pleasure of the nerve endings in my feet.

Ethan reaches for my hand. It's the first time he's done that when he wasn't pulling me through a window or reaching to comfort me in some dire place. This time he holds my hand for no purpose, just for joy.

I let the simple pleasure of my nerve endings extend to my hands, my fingers, to the places where my arm brushes against his. I pull us a little deeper into the water. I don't care that my sweatpants are getting wet. It feels nice. And anyway, I am a girl with a change of clothes.

We keep going like that until we are up to our waists, our clothes hanging heavy and my heart as light, I think, as it ever was or ever will be.

The first good-sized wave comes at us. I scream and he laughs and we both dive under it. We come up snorting and laughing.

We go farther out and just bob in the sunshine for a long time. I know there are scary things under the water, with chomping teeth and waving stinging arms, but I don't fear them. The surface of the water is too calm and lovely for me to believe in them right now.

Finally we drag our wet bodies back to the beach and lie down on the sand. We stay there for a long time, letting the warm air dry us slowly.

He lifts himself up onto one elbow and leans over me. He lets his fingers drift up my arm. He lifts my damp, salty tank top to my ribs and stares at these new parts of my body. He runs his hand over my hips and my belly button.

I try to keep breathing. 'You are going to make it harder on us when we have to stop,' I say to him.

'It's already harder,' he says.

He sits up, and I stare up at his strong back and the waist-band of his patched army-green pants. I've wanted to ask him about those pants so many times but shied away. When you ask someone a question, it's an invitation for them to ask you a question, and I could never afford that. It was one question of thousands I hadn't let myself ask.

I sit up too. 'Where do those pants come from?' It's such a forbidden delicacy, I can barely line up my words.

I guess Ethan is surprised too. 'What did you say?'

'Those pants. You always wear them.'

'Well . . .' He glances down at them. He's never looked remotely self-conscious about them before, but he does a little right now. 'My grandfather was a member of the Irish Defense Forces in the nineteen thirties and forties. These belonged to him.'

'Really.'

'Yeah. I have his cap badge too. His father, my great-grandfather, fought in the Irish War of Independence. He lost an arm. My dad's got his medals in the house somewhere.'

I nod. 'And your father?'

'He's an accountant at Ernst and Young.' He makes a slightly sour face.

'And your mom? She's a designer, right?' I am getting the hang of this, spending my questions like a millionaire.

'Exactly.' He shrugs. 'Her family was pretty amazing too.'

'In what way?'

He turns his face up to the sun. 'Her father was a Hungarian Jew. He and his wife were sent to the Nazi camps in 1944. My grandfather escaped early in 1945. He tried to save his wife, but she was already gone. He walked all the way across Europe, living in forests, wading across rivers, until he finally got to Paris. He worked for the resistance until the end of the war, and then he moved here.'

'Sad,' I say.

'But he made it. He remarried eventually – my grandmother – and started a business, had kids and grandkids.'

'Doesn't erase what he went through, though.'

'No. It doesn't. He's got the numbers on his arm to remind him.'

I hear myself sigh. I listen to the waves, probably my favorite sound in the world. 'Thanks,' I say.

He rolls onto his side. 'For what?'

'For letting me ask you questions. I've been wanting to for so long.'

'Anytime,' he says.

I put my hand out and Ethan takes it. He rolls onto his back and rests both our hands on top of his chest. For a long time I lose all my other thoughts in the up and down of his breathing.

Lying here like this, I can imagine happiness. Not a kicky, bright kind, but a full, almost aching kind, both dark and light. I can see the whole world in this way. I can imagine extending the feeling to other places and parts of the day. I can imagine holding it in my pocket like a lens, and bringing it out so that I can look through it and remember again and again the world that has this feeling in it.

FIFTEEN

In the hotel room after lunch we begin to put our strategy in place. Ethan calls the home number we found for Mona Ghali. He poses as a freelance IT guy, Jack Bonning, who works for her company. We'd sketched out the script in advance, during our drive down the coast.

'Ms. Ghali?' Ethan says. He lifts his eyebrows to tell me she's picked up. He pitches his voice low so she won't recognize him, and if I hadn't been nervous I might have laughed.

He gives her his fake name and identity with impressive matter-of-factness. I nod at him encouragingly.

'We've had some reports of hacking into the company server,' he explains, "so we're asking each of our employees to back up all files and temporarily move sensitive files to an alternate server.'

Ethan is a cool customer. I can't hear her part of the conversation, but he doesn't look troubled or stymied by any of what she says.

Ethan gives her the information for the alternate server. We'd figured on her uploading to a web server operated by her graduate department at MIT so she'd feel comfortable with it. It isn't actually an MIT server. Ethan is a decent programmer and a respectable hacker, but not like that. It has the markers of an MIT server, whereas it actually goes to an account set up by Ethan.

Ethan glances at me, which seems to mean it's working.

'And please do the same with all work files on your computer at home,' he adds before he hangs up.

I call Mona Ghali from our second phone forty-five minutes later, posing as a secretary from Human Resources. 'You might have heard we've been having some security issues,' I say. 'You've spoken to Mr. Bonning in IT?'

She replies that she has. I have the feeling she doesn't want to talk to me for any longer than necessary, and I get that. I try not to think too much, not to spook myself with the knowledge of what tomorrow has in store for her and for us.

'Well, it appears there have been a few files – physical files – that have gone missing from our offices here in Braintree, and we're concerned the same thing could be happening in the New Jersey office.'

'That's disturbing. I hadn't heard about that,' Mona Ghali says.

I go through the protocol Ethan and I invented, which involves locking her filing cabinets. I wait anxiously for her response.

'Yes, my files do have locks. I am not in the habit of using them, but I will start today,' she says.

For several minutes after I hang up my heart is still thumping. For a stretch there, I was really enjoying not lying.

That afternoon Ethan and I buy a cheap beach umbrella, change into proper bathing suits – or shorts in his case, which he had the forethought to pack in his duffel bag – steal a couple of towels from the hotel and sit under the umbrella, just a few yards up from the surf (and actually in the surf, at one point, when high tide catches us unawares).

We play cards. We play for a couple of hours, refining our next day's strategy along the way. The procedure goes like this: Ethan teaches me a new game and then we play it until I beat him, at which point he figures I am good enough and we go on to the next one. He doesn't like to get beaten, so we pass through Crazy Eights, Old Maid and Go Fish pretty quickly. It takes me five rounds to beat him at Spit, but it is extra sweet when I do. Bloody Knuckles involves several rounds of suffering, but when I finally win, he picks a queen, so I get to whack him on the knuckles with the deck of cards twelve times, and I do not hold back.

Ethan claims he is some kind of supergenius expert at Gin, so when I beat him in our second game, he is so beset by rage and disbelief that he makes us play three more times, and writhes in psychological pain as I beat him every time.

'I think I'm better at the skill games than the luck games,' I say.

'Oh, shut up,' he says. He shakes his head. 'I've created a monster.'

Ethan says his ego isn't up to teaching me Hearts quite yet, so we go swimming instead. The waves are getting big and I am not much of a swimmer. There was no voluntary swimming where I came from. For a million reasons, there just wasn't. I swam for the first time in a pool in a neighbor's backyard when I was twelve. But I don't want to be a chicken, so I follow Ethan out deep.

One wave takes me by surprise and almost steals my bathing suit bottoms. I turn away from Ethan, find the sand under my feet and walk a few steps toward the shore, trying to rearrange myself so the crucial parts of my body are covered.

I guess I should realize that the dramatic sucking of water behind me is going toward the assembly of an absolutely giant wave. I turn my head and see what is coming, but it is too late to go over or under it.

It hits me full in the back, tossing me forward and spinning me around like a sock in the washing machine. The spin cycle goes on for a long time.

I feel sand scratching along my back one moment and my cheek the next. I am so disoriented I can't figure out which direction the air is in. I am thinking what a stupid and embarrassing way this is to go – in about four feet of water – when I feel a hand reaching around my upper arm and pulling me in some direction, hopefully airward.

I turn my head toward the hand, get one of my feet under my body and at last suck in a lungful of oxygen. I cough and choke and stagger as Ethan leads me toward the shore.

He is shaking his head at me, but not completely without sympathy.

I push my hair out of my face and try to catch my breath.

As we stand in water ankle deep, Ethan puts both hands on my waist. When I look up at him, he leans his head down and kisses my salty lips.

That's all it is. He drops his hands and we walk out of the water and up to our beach umbrella.

Thankfully, my bathing suit is mostly in the right vicinity. I straighten it. I touch the scratches on my cheek and rub the stinging backs of my hands. I still feel the kiss. I don't know what to do.

'What's the matter?' he asks, looking me over for injuries, challenging me to deny him that kiss. I can't do it.

'My knuckles hurt,' I say.

Early that evening in our hotel room I lie on the rubbery bedspread, tapping various searches into the laptop Ethan brought along and watching the pink late-sunset light creep across the floor. This is the day I don't want to end. Ethan is lying a foot or so away, looking through near-future newspapers.

I've spent a long time on Mona Ghali's social networking pages, taking notes and memorizing details for tomorrow. Ethan was already her friend on Facebook, which makes things simpler.

Because Ethan's computer is logged on to his Facebook page, I can't help but notice all the hundreds of friends he has and the constant posts from happy, carefree teenagers. And I can't help thinking, *What does he want with me? Why would he leave that to go on this mind-warping odyssey?*

I rest my chin on my hand and look at him. 'What are you missing to be here?'

He looks up from the papers. He lifts his eyebrows. 'What am I missing? Nothing.'

I tip my head toward him. 'You know. You've got a whole life. You're a normal person. What would you be doing if you weren't here?'

'Well, let's see.' I can tell by his face he's humoring me. 'Tonight is my mom's book group. I am missing eight middle-aged ladies and a lot of chardonnay.'

'Really?' I laugh.

'I am missing some moping from my dad, who doesn't enjoy ladies' book group night, and greasy Chinese takeout. He'd try to get me to go see a violent and manly movie with him.'

'And would you?'

'Maybe. Jamie Webb invited me to a Yankees game. Veronique Lasser is having a party, I think.'

I can't help but feel wistful. 'That sounds nice.'

He shrugs. 'I'm a Mets fan, and Veronique's parties are never fun.' He reaches out and takes my bare foot in his hand. 'You know where I want to be tonight?'

I'm like a starving person at a banquet. 'Where?'

'Here.'

'Yeah?'

'Nowhere else.'

'Yeah?'

'Yeah.'

'Me too.'

We get back to work.

I keep searching for Andrew Baltos on the Web and finding nothing. He seems like somebody who's good at self-deleting. Finally I get off the bed and retrieve the red folder from the safe. I flop back down. Ethan is still deep in the newspapers. I touch my toe to his knee, just because I can.

'Don't get me started, Jamesie,' he warns me, not looking up from his paper.

'I know. Sorry. We're working.' Even so, I feel his hand settle just inside the waistband of my shorts. We are not making it easy.

The first thing I do is go to Theresa Hunt's Facebook

profile page. It hasn't been updated in a few months, and I wonder if she's okay. Aimlessly I scroll through her pictures. I see pictures of her with her son, who seems like the right age to be Jason Hunt.

'You finding anything?' Ethan asks me.

'Not so far. I'm not sure what I'm looking for. You?'

'Just freaking myself out, mainly.'

I scroll down through her pictures to when Jason was a baby. Theresa looked young and happy then. I go back farther and then I stop. I take a breath. I click on a picture. I'm not sure I totally trust my eyes yet. I slide the computer toward Ethan. 'Who does that look like to you? The man standing next to Theresa.'

He looks at it closely and then sizes it back down. 'Do you think it's Andrew Baltos?'

My heart is starting to thump. 'Do you?'

He looks again. He scrolls down farther. 'There's another one of him. It's tagged. It says Andrew.'

'I really think it's him.'

'Who is she, though?' Ethan asks.

'She's the first person documented in that red folder. He wrote "Patient Number One" on her page with a question mark. I think my father was trying to trace the earliest cases of what later became the blood plague.

I cannot figure out what she could have to do with Andrew Baltos.'

Ethan keeps looking through the pictures. 'I think they were a couple. That's how it looks.'

'It does. Wow.' In one of the pictures they are in full PDA. 'That's not very complicated.' My mind is jumping around. 'So what does it mean? Maybe she gave the illness to Andrew Baltos.' I'm trying to figure out the timing; in the early phases the disease had a much longer incubation period. 'But what does that have to do with Mona Ghali? Does Mona Ghali get sick too? Does the murder have something to do with that? I thought she was targeted because of her energy research. All the stuff he took from her computer.'

'But it can't be a coincidence. Can it?'

'No. I don't know.' I put my head down on the bed. It's tiring. 'I don't think so.'

'Maybe that was the angle your father was working.'

'But I'm not sure he discovered the connection to Mona Ghali's murder.'

'So we're getting somewhere, right?'

'Yes.' I push the computer away and lie on my back. I put my hands over my face. 'I kind of wish I knew where.'

Ethan rolls on top of me. How long could we lie on a bed together and not let that happen? I put my arms around him. I feel his shoulders, his back. 'Is this a good idea?' I ask, a tiny bit suffocated.

'Yes.' He puts an elbow down next to my head to relieve a little weight. 'It's a great idea.' He leans his head down to mine and kisses me long and deeply. I want it so much it scares me. I push him off. I sit up.

'Ethan, it's not. We can't.'

He sits up too. 'Here's what I want to know. Why do you believe anything they say? What makes you think this business about you hurting me is not another lie to keep you scared and isolated? Why should this be different from everything else they say?'

'It could be a lie. I've thought of that.' I put my hand on his thigh. 'But what if it's not?' My voice is strained. 'I come from an awful place and you come from this lovely one. I am so scared of what I brought from there putting you in danger. We've already done too much.'

He kneels over my legs and puts both of his hands on my face. His eyes are serious on mine. 'Listen, Prenna. Do you know how long I've loved you? Being with you is not going to hurt me. I refuse to believe it.'

'But what if—'

'And you know what the truth is?'

'What?'

'If I could make love to you right now, I wouldn't mind if I died.'

My eyes are teary, but I can't help smiling. 'Well, I would mind. I really would.'

We eat dinner on the patio of a Mexican restaurant spangled with twinkling white lights. Ethan brandishes his fake ID and comes back with a pitcher of sangria.

We are happily chowing down our enchiladas suizas when a mosquito lands on Ethan's arm. I am not prepared for the adrenaline that bursts through my bloodstream. Without thinking, I fling out my hand and smack it with the wrath of Satan.

Ethan looks stunned and almost fearful.

'Sorry,' I say. My head swims. Maybe the sangria isn't a great idea. I am too emotional tonight to begin with. I look at my hand with the smeared bug and hold it up for him. 'Got it.'

He opens his eyes wide. 'I'll say. I hope my arm's not broken.'

I get up and put my napkin on the table. 'I'll be right back,' I say. I go to the bathroom and wash the remains of the vile creature down the sink. I scrub my hands with soap.

I look at myself in the mirror and see tears in my eyes.

I feel strangely off balance. What business do I have being happy? Falling in love? Thinking I know what happiness is?

I go back to the table. I try to arrange my face back into my beach girl persona, but there is no point.

'Are you okay?' Ethan asks, his eyes reading mine astutely, as they usually do.

'Yeah. I guess. Sorry about your arm.'

'Was it the mosquito?' he asks. His face is concerned.

I put my elbow on the table and rest my head in my hand. The enchiladas, which had seemed purely delicious a few minutes before, look nauseating. 'Yes, sort of.'

He doesn't pester me with questions. He waits to see what I'm ready to say.

I guess I'm ready to say a lot, because I open my mouth and all kinds of things come out.

'I used to have two younger brothers,' I say. 'They died in the plague. My brother Julius was two years younger than me. I was closer to him than anyone else. He was almost seven when he died, and the little one, Remus, was just a baby.'

Ethan reaches for my hand.

'That wasn't the baby's name officially. At least, not according to my mother. People stopped naming their babies in the worst plague years because so many of them died, but my father made each of us a birth certificate with an official name, and insisted on using them even in the days after my brothers died.'

'Your mother didn't?' Ethan asks.

I shake my head. 'Since we came here my mother has referred to them a handful of times at most, and never said their names. I understand. Her heart was broken too.'

Ethan looks devastated. His face reflects the expression he must see on mine.

'I remember seeing the red swollen spot on Remus's cheek with absolute dread. The plague had taken other people's brothers and sisters and parents, but it hadn't come to my house yet. Nobody saw the mosquito that bit Remus. There were screens everywhere, and we all slept and sat under nets. We zipped our nets and sprayed our toxic sprays and said our prayers, because mosquitoes carried death. It's hard to unlearn it, even now. By then, you know, the world was a lot wetter and a lot hotter. Every worry and unhappiness in the world, and there were a lot of them, took the form of the mosquito.'

I close my eyes. I gather a picture and then I push it away.

'I obsessed over that red spot on the baby's cheek. It could have been a pimple or some other kind of bite, my mother said. But on the fourth day the telltale symptoms started – the fever and the rash and the red eyes. Remus was still smiling then. He had no idea what was overtaking him. That nearly killed me. And there was nothing we could do.'

He squeezes my hand.

I am surprised by the stuff I am remembering. I guess memory is a deep well, and you don't know what's down there until you lower the bucket and start hauling it up. 'It wasn't anything out of the ordinary. That's the thing. You couldn't feel sorry for yourself. It was happening everywhere. You couldn't let it pull you under, because you didn't know what was next, whether it would be your mother or your father or you. Looking back, you can see the complete arc of tragedy where each thing sat, but in the moment it is just panic. Was it the beginning? Was it the end? Were you about to die, or were you supposed to get through it alive? You kind of wished for neither. I knew a kid who lost both of his parents in a day. He sat on the floor of his house with the bodies. He didn't know what to do.'

'Jesus,' Ethan says.

'You weren't supposed to touch the victims after the plague symptoms began. You were supposed to quarantine them and then get rid of the bodies as quick as possible. Even before it was carried by mosquitoes, it could be passed from person to person.' I rushed on, because I knew if I stopped talking, I would not know how to start again. 'Of course people were terrified of spending time in public places, touching each other and taking care of sick people. Our neighbor was a medic, one of the rare survivors of the disease and supposedly immune. He took the baby away to let him die in his yard along with dozens of others. I couldn't let him go. I couldn't stand the idea of our baby going with a stranger. I chased the neighbor and took the baby back. I guess I was eight. I kept him in our yard, and he died in my arms. I didn't care if I died too.'

Ethan's face seems to absorb my sorrow. He shakes his head. 'But you didn't get it.'

'No. That poor neighbor died within the month, but I think I really was immune. The night I held the baby I got stung by a mosquito. I didn't tell anybody about it; I just waited to die. Maybe I wanted to. But I didn't.'

He looks sad. He puts his head down.

'My brother Julius did.' I look up at the sky, the brightness of the stars dimmed and blurred by the bright beach lights. I can't say anything more about that.

Impatiently I wipe the tears from my eyes. 'When I really want to torture myself, I picture Remus's smile on that day when he first got sick.'

Ethan shakes his head. 'Why would you want to torture yourself?'

I don't need to think to answer. 'Because I'm here and he's not. Because I lived.'

◆ SIXTEEN

I take a scalding shower. I brush my teeth to an extravagant degree. I try to enjoy the simple pleasures of clean hair and unworn clothes. Ethan holds me for a moment when I come out of the bathroom in my towel. 'No more sand in my ears.'

He laughs, but I can tell he's being careful. A story like the one I told can really bring down the mood.

I see that he's made up the scratchy-looking couch with a sheet, a pillow and a blanket. 'It doesn't fold out?' I ask.

'No. It turns out not. That's okay,' he says brightly.

It is really more a love seat than a couch. I am tall and Ethan is taller. He is going to have to fold himself in half to fit on it.

I look guiltily at the vast bed. 'Are you sure?'

'Yes. No problem at all.'

'I hear you are really good at sleeping sitting up.'

He laughs again and goes into the bathroom. I listen to him brushing his teeth.

I turn off the main overhead light. I unwrap the towel and pull on a tank top and a pair of fresh underwear. I strip off the rubbery bedspread and get under the crisp white sheets and blanket. I turn my head on the pillow and search with my excellent eyes through the balcony doors for our partial ocean view.

Ethan emerges from the bathroom in his boxer shorts. He turns off the last lamp, and I watch with pity as he contorts himself to fit onto the little couch.

I lie there thinking of what to say. I prop myself up on my elbow. 'After the story I told tonight, do you still want to share a bed with me?'

He's instantly up and out of the couch. 'The most of anything.'

I lift the covers and he climbs into bed, covering my body with his. I don't think I've ever felt anything nicer. 'After the story I told tonight, we're keeping it casual, Ethan Jarves,' I whisper to his cheek.

'Awwww. *Please.*'

'No, or it's back to the couch.'

'Fine, then, cruel girl.'

Bit by bit I feel his hands searching around my body, pushing up under my tank top.

'Ethan,' I whisper. I put my hands over his. 'If this is casual, what do you call intimate?'

'I was just about to show you that.'

I shouldn't laugh. 'Back to the couch.'

'Fine. Fine.'

I wake up with the first light of the sun. I try to draw out the moment as long as possible. So many mornings I've woken with the burden of reassimilating sadness and loss. This morning I assimilate joy. I take in Ethan's bed hair, his scent, the freckles on his shoulders, the feeling of his legs tangled with mine. I don't want even the tiniest tendril of it to get away from me.

But eventually I have to pee. I gently extricate my various bits and parts from his. Luckily, he's a deep and happy sleeper. I sit on the edge of the bed for an extra moment and admire the freedom of his sprawl. It's hard not to touch him, now that I can. It's difficult to separate my body from his.

I go to the bathroom and brush my teeth. Quietly I take the newspapers from the safe and sit on the floor by the French doors to the balcony, where the most light comes in. From the paper dated tomorrow I reread the first article about the death of Mona Ghali, and then other articles in the section – one about a fatal car accident in Ossining killing a father and two children, another about a house fire in Montclair.

I think about finding the number of the driver from Ossining and calling him. I couldn't tell him what I know, obviously – he'd never believe me – but I could come up with some clever way of keeping him off the roads that night. I wouldn't have to call him at all. I could puncture a tire or put sugar in his gas tank. I could take matters into my own hands.

And the people whose house burned down? I could anonymously report a dangerous electrical situation and try to get a fire inspector sent over to the house. I could pose as a fire inspector over the phone and get them to at least put fresh batteries in their smoke detectors.

I am suddenly the vigilante future girl, star of my own not-very-glorious superhero comic strip.

Naturally, I think of the fourth rule. It is among the most serious of them. It isn't the rule the counselors talk about most, but somehow it still has more natural weight than the others.

I turn to the last page of the paper, with the obituaries

in small print. Some of them have a few lines about the person's life or death, and most not much more than dates and the names of the family members who survive them. Most of the dead are old people, probably sick people, whose deaths you could do nothing to prevent. But what about the other ones?

It's an intoxicating power to think about, saving people from death, preventing tragedy, swooping in at some critical juncture to make sure a life goes in one direction instead of another.

What if there were other moments, less than death but still important, when you could tip the balance just a little in an instance of defeat or discouragement. I guess it would be hard to find those moments in the newspaper.

With my finger I move down the list of deaths to the youngest near the bottom. *January 2, 1996–May 17, 2014.* My eyes stick on that date. I feel a chill starting in the bottom of my abdomen. I move my finger across the column to the left. *Ethan Patrick Jarves, beloved son.* I tear my eyes from the newspaper, disoriented. I feel my vision, my excellent vision, go out of focus. This isn't possible.

I look across the room at that very beloved son, beloved friend, beloved beloved, sprawled over the bed we shared, as tanned and strong and healthy as a beloved could be.

That cannot be. I look back down at the paper, actually expecting to see something different this time, but it's the same.

Ethan Patrick Jarves, beloved son. Survived by his parents and his sister.

My eyes feel like they are vibrating in their sockets. My heart is thrashing like a prisoner in my chest.

Ethan makes a sleeping noise and kicks his leg out from under the sheet.

I jump to my feet, holding the paper. I go to the bathroom as quietly as possible, pull on shorts and let myself out of the room. I walk toward the elevators. I still can't see right.

Clutching the newspaper, I make my way out of the lobby and down the path to the beach. I walk to the little rise before the water. It is still early and the beach is mostly empty but for gulls picking at the overflowing garbage cans.

I fold the newspaper many times so it won't blow around. I still think I could give it another chance, that when I open it again, it will say different things, and beloved Ethan Patrick Jarves will be nowhere in it.

It isn't real. It hasn't happened yet. It is one possible

future, and there are infinite other possibilities. This is not going to be the future. I don't believe it.

And even though I don't believe it, my mind spins around and around it. How does he die? What is the cause? It's the same day as the death of Mona Ghali, so is it linked to that? Because the future this newspaper describes is not the future I am part of. I was not here yet and neither was my father. It could not include the possibility that Ethan and I would team up to intervene in a murder.

The version of the future where Ethan dies on May 17 can't have to do with me. What about Mona Ghali, though? He knows her. He often goes to that lab.

I wish I had more information. I don't have any other newspapers from the future to cross-reference. I can't investigate a death before it happens.

I realize I am crying. Tears roll down my face, drip on the folded newspaper and on the back of my hand.

Can't I keep anything I love?

I watch the water for a long time when Ethan, beloved, appears next to me. I've dried my eyes by then.

'You got up early,' he says accusingly. 'I don't like waking up and not feeling you there.' He laughs at himself. 'Sorry. I got used to you.'

I stand up and boldly put my arms around him. It's not really so bold – I mostly don't want him to see my face. 'I did get up early,' I say. 'I wanted you to sleep.'

He kisses me on the neck and behind my ear and then, in open rebellion, on my mouth. 'Have I mentioned,' he says a little breathlessly, 'that I don't feel a bit sick? That I've never felt better in my life?'

I smile. I want to look happy.

'Just saying.'

Everything is breaking my heart.

'They've got an all-you-can-eat breakfast buffet this morning. You want to go?' He says it like we've won a prize.

'Yes, okay,' I say. I am still afraid of what his eyes will find on my face.

He is so enthusiastic over the buffet it makes my heart hurt. He helps himself to four giant waffles, two doughnuts, a bowl of granola, a cup of yogurt, a side plate of sausage and bacon, a tall glass of milk and a glass of orange juice.

'Henny, they have these little chocolate éclairs,' he shouts to me joyously across the restaurant.

I put an éclair and a few pieces of fruit on my plate,

knowing it will be a struggle to eat any of it.

We have most of the place to ourselves. We sit at a table for two by the window from which you can see the ocean. The water is especially bright, the color of mint mouthwash.

'This is our day,' Ethan says between bites of waffle.

Last night I was excited to take on our day. Now my heart is plunging.

'We should take off after breakfast and get close to Teaneck by early afternoon.' He spears a sausage. 'And during our downtime, I'm going to teach you Hearts.'

'We've got to have our priorities,' I say.

'We do. Because once you've got Hearts down, you're set.'

'And then I'll be a proper early-twenty-first-century girl?' I ask. I feel like crying. I don't want to be set.

'Yes, ma'am.'

'But there's got to be something else you can teach me. You can't be done with me yet.'

He stops chewing for a moment and looks at me carefully. 'Are you kidding? Not even close. There are plenty of things I am going to teach you.'

I watch him eat nearly all of the all-you-can-eat buffet, most of it with a dot of syrup on his chin, and I make a vow to myself.

I will not let him die. No matter what it takes. I don't care about any version of the future besides the one I am making, where Ethan is not going to die because I am not going to let him.

◆ SEVENTEEN

Ethan watches the road and I watch Ethan. I'm scared to take my eyes off him. He turns his head briefly to glance at me.

'You okay?'

Should I tell him? I twist my fingers together. Maybe I should, but I can't. Putting the words into the air would give them a degree of reality I won't allow. As it is, it's an idea that exists only between me and a tiny line of print in a soon-to-be-inaccurate newspaper. Nobody else needs to know.

And anyway, what if knowing it made Ethan feel fatalistic and hopeless? Or what if he tried so vigorously to make it not come true that it came true in spite of him?

No, I can't say the words. Since I am the only one

who knows them and I love him to the point of agony, I will be his guardian today.

I force myself to stop staring at him. Now my excellent eyes are ticking along the exits of the Garden State Parkway, seeing strange poetry in the place names: Manahawkin, Forked River, Island Heights, Pleasant Plains, Asbury Park, Neptune. Something occurs to me.

'Can you turn off?' I say.

'At this exit?'

'Yes.'

'Here?'

I am reading all the signs I can find. 'Yes, I think it's here.'

Ethan turns. 'What's here?'

I am spinning in my seat, one way and then the other. 'I recognize some of the names. It looks different, though.'

'Okay.' Ethan pulls up to an intersection. 'Which way?'

I study the signs. I try to think. 'Left. Maybe.'

'Left maybe it is.'

'Keep going,' I say.

He drives for a mile or so, and I have this memory. 'Turn right here.'

'Okay.'

'Now keep going.' I am up on my knees in the seat.

'Right there. Do you see that?'

'The school?'

'Yes. Can you stop?'

Ethan pulls up and parks in front. It's Saturday, so it's empty.

'I can't believe it,' I say in a low voice, getting out of the car.

Ethan follows me across the grass to the top of a little hill where you can see the playground spreading from the back of the school.

'Do you know what this is?'

'I really don't.'

'This was the local elementary school where we lived. Before, I mean. Before we emigrated.'

Ethan's eyes open wide. 'Really? Right here?'

'I'm almost sure.' Blossoming trees dot the schoolyard, and the sunshine is soft on our heads. The memories associated with the school are unnerving, but the place itself feels oddly comforting. It gives a sense of continuity to my life that I almost never feel.

I realize I want to stay here. Because what bad thing could happen to Ethan here? We could sit on the grass all day and watch the clouds and the birds. There'd be no danger of highway accidents or murders gone awry. I could keep my arms around him until the day is over.

'Did you go to this school?' he asks, holding my hand.

'No. I would have. I wanted to. It got shut down right before I would have started kindergarten. They said temporarily, but it never reopened.' Down goes the bucket again, into the long-abandoned memory well. I surprise myself with what comes up.

Ethan has his curious but careful look. 'Where did you go to school?'

'I didn't. We were homeschooled. My dad took it very seriously. You tease me about my superbrain. It was just my dad being a teacher with nowhere else to teach and us kids not being allowed outside.'

'Your dad was a great teacher.'

I nod. 'He was. But still I wanted to go to this school *so bad*. I read all these books where kids went to school. I was always pretending.'

'What year did they close it?'

'The first real plague year was '87. There were rumblings of the epidemic for years, but they kept beating it back and containing it. It wasn't until mosquitoes started spreading it that hell broke loose.'

'2087.'

'Yes. I think they closed it during the second one in '91.'

'So you were . . . five, about?'

'Yeah.'

He lifts his eyebrows as he considers this. 'You know, you're kind of young for me.'

I laugh. 'And you're older than my grandmother.'

'You were born around here?'

'Not far.'

'It was still the US by then?'

'Yes. I am not an illegal alien. Not in that way.'

'So the country was still going, at least.'

'Yes. Not going well.'

He looks sad.

'Nor was any other one, really,' I say. 'Not that that's a big consolation.'

'And when did you leave?'

'We left in 2098 and arrived in 2010.'

'Why then?'

'Why 2098? I guess that was the first moment they figured out the technology to make the time path work so we could get out. My dad used to tell me about how all through the late twenty seventies and eighties there was a race to find another place to go. By then most everybody knew the planet was becoming uninhabitable pretty quickly.'

'I guess at a certain point, nobody can deny it anymore.'

'A few scientists held out for a really long time, and they had a lot of eager followers – whether out of optimism or cynicism I'm not sure – but they came to look ridiculous as the problems got worse and worse.'

I listen to myself talk, almost as if it's a separate Prenna carrying on this conversation. On some level, I think I understand what separate-Prenna is doing. If she keeps talking, maybe Ethan won't notice we aren't getting any closer to Teaneck, New Jersey.

So separate-Prenna forges on. 'Some doctors and scientists were trying to fix the problems, but most knew it was too late for that; they were just trying to figure out a way to escape. There were plans to colonize the moon, Mars, a space station. There were big ambitious plans, but not enough time. People were dying. The only colonization scheme that worked was the simplest – colonizing the past.'

'How many times was the path used?'

'Until a couple of days ago, I would have said once. But it had to have been used again for my father to have gotten here.'

'To 2010.'

'Yes. I can't even imagine what the world was like by the time he left.'

'Maybe there were other times too.'

I shiver. 'There's the legend of Traveler One. Not that anybody believes it.'

'Who's Traveler One?'

'Every one of us has a number, from our chief counselor, Traveler Two, to my mother to me – Traveler 971, by the way – to Ashley Myers, the youngest, Traveler 996. Traveler One supposedly used the path first and learned the ways of time. He was like our Moses. He handed down the twelve rules.'

'And then they retired his number.'

'Right.'

'So that means he's around here somewhere.'

'If he exists and everybody comes out in 2010, then he must be.'

'I could have seen him in the woods too.'

'I doubt it, though. I suspect he's what you politely call a "metaphor". They invented him to give legitimacy to the rules. So it wouldn't seem like they were just making shit up.'

We walk around to the back of the school to the little playground I played there only a few times before it was dismantled. They didn't want to be tempting kids outside.

'You know what surprises me most?' I say as we each sit down on a swing.

'What?'

'That everybody knows.'

Ethan kicks at the dirt under his swing. 'What do you mean?'

'Everybody here knows what's going to happen. Before we came here, I imagined that people in the late twentieth and early twenty-first centuries must have been ignorant of what they were doing to the world, because how else could they have kept on doing it? But they do know. They don't know exactly how it will unfold, but they know a lot.'

'We do know, don't we?'

'People from the twenty eighties look back on this period now and the one just ahead as the golden age of science. As the golden age of a lot of things, actually. You can't imagine the nostalgia for this exact time. The science was good enough to predict a century ahead what was going to happen. And it's not just a handful of scientists who know, it's everybody. I read about it, hear about it, see it on the news practically every day. There couldn't be any more warning.'

'Not everybody ignores it.'

'No, that's true. But people here have strange ideas about what to do to help. There is Earth Day and all kinds of green products that make people feel good – as though organic cotton sheets and hemp socks are going to do the trick. But nobody does the hard things. Not if it costs them anything. Nobody calls for any real sacrifices. Politicians aren't very brave. I mean, eventually they will demand sacrifices – they'll have to, there will be no choice – but by then it will be too late.'

He looks distraught. 'So that's what happens.'

'That's what happens.'

He is quiet for a long time. 'And your leaders know all this and aren't doing anything about it?'

'The opposite. They're making sure nobody does. You read my father's letter. When we got here, they acted like they were the Founding Fathers of the USA or something, bold and innovative. I believed it at first, but it wasn't true. Everything they did was for secrecy and manipulation – they created birth certificates, passports, credit reports, family histories. Even old family photos. They tried to block out memories of our old life, but it didn't really work. Except for the trip itself and a day or two afterward, I remember almost everything. And then they tried to retrain us for our lives here, packing a whole childhood's worth of adaptation into a couple of years. They were thorough, but they still missed a few things.' I chew on my bottom lip. 'Like teaching us card games, for instance.'

Ethan smiles at me and I smile back. He pumps his legs to get his swing going, and I pump mine. I think I would like to stay here on these swings together until midnight, possibly until the end of my life.

'And they missed a very big thing, which was freedom. We had secrets to keep and scripts to follow, but no freedom at all. I don't think Benjamin Franklin would have approved of that.'

'No. Not much.'

'It's possible there might have been a little more idealism at first, but when they found how comfortable and safe and nice it is here, I think whatever they had of it was lost. They turned us into parasites. They rely on the future too much to want to change it.'

'Even though . . .'

'Even though.' I shrug. 'For a long time I wanted to trust them. The community was my whole world – many of them I like and some I love. They all go along with what the leaders say, or at least they try. But I can't anymore. They are as complacent, shortsighted and selfish as everybody else. And a lot more corrupt.'

'God, that's depressing.'

'But the thing is, no one really believes in the future, do they? It's like believing in your own death. You can't do it. Nobody can. Not even us, who have seen it with our eyes.'

Of course my mind pulls up the tiny, hateful line of

print in tomorrow's paper. Another death I don't, can't, won't believe.

He is quiet for a moment. 'Does your mother still trust them?'

'She doesn't go against them, I can say that much. I don't know if that's out of consent or fear.'

'Do you think she knew about your father?'

'I don't think so.' I close my eyes. 'I'd really rather tell myself she didn't.' I run my finger along the rusted chain. 'My mother went through a lot, you know. They say suffering makes you stronger and wiser, but I'm worried that more often it makes you weaker and more scared. She wants us to be safe for another hour, another day. That's what she cares about.'

'That's a sad thought. That's probably what most people care about,' Ethan says.

I stare at him and I want to cry. I realize how true it is. I'm weak and scared too. Because of that line of print in the newspaper, that's what I care about too.

'But you are different, because you know how much that hour costs,' he says solemnly. 'And now I am different too. We know what happens if we do nothing.'

I wipe my nose on my sleeve. I want to be different. But now I am afraid.

He times our swings to catch my hand and holds it

until we are swinging in unison. You get the feeling nobody ever denied him a playground.

He expertly stops the swinging and pulls me up before I can get my balance. He is dragging me purposefully back in the direction of the car. 'Until today,' he says. 'That is what today is all about.'

And I know he's right. We have to keep going.

'Wasn't there anything cool? Wasn't there anything great?' Ethan asks me somewhere between Asbury Park and Freehold.

I want to give him everything he wants, tell him everything he ever wanted to know. He's stifled his curiosity for a long time. I just wish the news were better.

He casts a look at me. 'You don't have to tell me now. No hurry. I plan to be asking you questions for the next seventy to eighty years.'

What an ache that gives me. I can barely swallow down the feeling. 'I heard about some cool things,' I say, trying to loosen up my throat for the words to come through. 'I saw a few of them, but mostly they weren't working so well by the time I was born. Computing technology by the late teens and early twenties was totally released from boxes and screens, keyboards and mice.

Images could be almost anywhere, on screens thin as paper or soft as a curtain or just projected into the air in front of you. You manipulated information and images directly with your hands, your eyes, even your mind in some cases.'

Ethan nods keenly, happily. 'You can see all that coming,' he says.

'One cool thing was this app that makes you disappear. I never really saw one work, but I read about them in stories written in the twenties and thirties. I think they are perfecting the technology now – where sensors read the contours of your body as you move and project the background onto you so you blend in seamlessly with your surroundings.'

'I've read about that,' Ethan says. He glances at me again. 'It's funny to hear you talk about the future as the past. Or strange, anyway.'

'I know it is. I always have a hard time with sense.'

'So what else?'

'Well, there was a lot of R and D money and scientific genius spent on pills and simple surgeries to let people eat as much as they wanted without getting fat. And there were big advances in plastic surgery technology, so people could shape their bodies exactly how they wanted and look super young, even when they were, like, seventy. I think it got to be pretty creepy, to tell you the truth.'

Ethan's face is sober. 'What a waste. And meanwhile the world is falling apart.'

'Almost all of that craziness petered out by the end of the forties. And it's really ironic, because the serious food shortages started in the fifties, and for the majority of people even in this country, being fat was no longer an option.'

Ethan shakes his head. 'That's just sad.'

I can hear Poppy's voice describing these things, impassioned at the kitchen table. I think of the old man in the dark under the table in the community center, telling me about the fork. I still can't hear my Poppy in that voice.

'So what if today, tonight, really is the fork?' Ethan says. 'How is it going to change the story? Is Mona Ghali's research that important, do you think? I doubt it will fix the fat pills.'

I've been thinking about that too. 'Her research is energy.'

'Yeah. She's working on capturing the energy of ocean surface waves.'

'And if it works?'

Ethan considers. 'Why don't you tell me how the

story goes. Starting around now.'

I should know all this by heart. These were the cautionary tales Poppy loved to teach. 'Okay, so as of now the weather patterns for growing food are still pretty stable, as they have been for a long time, and people take it for granted. You have the Gulf Stream warming up Europe, and there are rainy places and dry places. Right?'

'Right.'

'But then everything starts to change, more or less as they predict. The ice caps melting, the ice sheets collapsing, the water levels rising. It's slow enough at first that people think they can adapt. I remember seeing the ruins of some pretty crazy sea walls people tried to build in the forties. But then it just accelerates. The whole thing changes over about fifteen years. There are droughts and floods and storms that rip the topsoil right off the earth. Once people recover from one thing, there is another. The price of basic stuff like wheat and rice skyrockets, and governments come down because they can't feed people.' I look up. I realize I'm talking in a rush. 'So there you have it: your quickie history. The decline of humankind in under one minute.'

'And then the mosquito.'

'Skipping ahead about twenty, thirty years, but yes.'

'That's at least partly a climate issue too.'

'Definitely it is.'

'So if Mona's figuring out a clean, cheap energy source that doesn't release any carbon, that's a huge deal.'

'Yes.'

'And if Mona's the one who's going to patent this at a US lab, then maybe it helps fix the finances of this country, not having to buy all that oil, but instead having some technology to export.'

'Would be nice if we had some other, better future to compare it to, but it does sound plausible.'

'Doesn't help with the fat pills, though.'

'Well, we can't ask Mona to fix everything.'

Ethan is thoughtful for a moment. 'What if the future doesn't want to be changed? What if it wants what it wants? What if it makes no difference what any of us do, whether we are heroes or cowards?'

I hate this thought. On this day of days, I am so scared of it I won't even think it. 'The future doesn't *want* anything,' I say, a little too forcefully. 'We're the ones who make the future.' That's what I want to believe, anyway.

I think of Ethan and our eighty years of questions. I think of Poppy and how much he sacrificed for this.

◆ EIGHTEEN

Ethan insists on teaching me to play Hearts over floppy French fries and terrible hamburgers at a rest stop on the Garden State Parkway. Ethan eats his heartily. He puts down the wrapper with a sigh. I can hardly choke down a bite of mine.

'That was the worst bacon cheeseburger I ever ate,' he says, 'but it was still a bacon cheeseburger.'

We've got six hours before our date with destiny. I am not quite the quick study at cards I was yesterday. I find myself watching Ethan's mouth, his fingers, his forearms, his chin.

'Okay, so what would you lead this time?' he asks avidly.

The cards are a blur in my hand.

'The, um, ten?'

'Of diamonds? No! You don't want to lose your shot at the jack of diamonds right away. Try again.'

I nod. I wish I weren't getting an ulcer. I wish I could concentrate. 'This one?' I pull out a four of clubs.

'I guess that could make it around with only three hands playing. You can try it.'

I wish I knew what he was talking about. I put down the four and he immediately slaps a seven of hearts on it.

I look at his eyelashes, which any girl would envy. 'That's bad, right?' I say.

'Yes. Hearts are points. They are bad. You don't want to get stuck with any points.'

'No points. Got it.' I look at my hand. I look at his ear. I study the scattering of freckles over his nose.

'Hearts are bad,' he reiterates. 'The queen of spades is very bad. Points are bad. You want to end each hand with as few points as possible.'

I nod dejectedly. 'I think I like games where you try to win things better than the ones where you try not to win things.'

He gives me a flash of a smile. 'That's my girl,' he says. 'And that's why Hearts is the best game ever.'

I am unconvinced.

'Because the regular way to win, the way everyone tries to win Hearts, is by not getting any points, not winning any tricks, and going along as quietly and unobtrusively as you possibly can. That's how people win ninety-nine percent of the time.'

'Okay,' I say.

He lifts his eyebrows. 'But there's another way to win, a much bigger, much bolder way that a lot of Hearts players have never even dared to try. And when you win this way, you crush everyone else and prove that you are a boss.'

I do love his smile. I try to look more enthusiastic.

'It's called shooting the moon, and I'll teach it to you later.'

'Why later? Why not now?'

'Maybe my devastatingly fine looks are to blame, but it's because right now you aren't paying any attention to the cards.'

We park outside a bakery in Teaneck, New Jersey, at 5:55. The plan is for Ethan to go in and get a cake, and I am miserable with anxiety. I advise him not to get Mona's name in icing or anything; that would be going a bit far.

The plan is for me to do some more research, to make a couple of calls, but I don't want to lose sight of him for even this long. What if something happens to him in there? A bakery-related fatality? Would fortune be that nasty?

I hate not telling Ethan about what I read. I hate having any division between us. But I can't put it into the air either. My new ulcer is acting up. My spirits are low and I am having trouble keeping myself steady.

Ethan looks at me as he turns off the engine. 'You okay, Pren?'

'Oh.' I shrug. 'I was just thinking about . . . you know.'

'About poor Mona Ghali.'

I nod.

'And the fact that she has no idea what's coming.'

Aghast, I look at Ethan. I can't help it. 'Do you think we need to tell her?' I ask.

'If you think that's the best way to protect her.'

'I don't know, maybe not. But I hate knowing something about her that she doesn't know about herself. Maybe she could say important things to the people she loves. Just in case.'

Ethan agrees. 'I would want that, I guess.'

'Would you?'

'Yes. But I hesitate because I don't think she'd believe it. It would take too long to convince her even if we could, and if we couldn't, she probably wouldn't trust us enough to let us help her after that. She'd probably file for a restraining order or something.'

I hold my hands together so he won't see them shaking. I swallow and try to even out my voice. 'What would you want to do, if it were you?'

'If it were me?' He is tempted to say something clever, I think, but then he looks at my stricken face and changes his mind. 'Seriously?'

'Yes.'

'If I knew I was supposed to die?'

'Yes.'

He thinks for a while and levels me with a look. 'Are you sure you want me to tell you the truth?'

I nod, pressing my lips together.

He seems to gauge my tolerance for sincerity. 'Okay, well, since you insist. If I were going to die, there would be nothing to keep me from you – from all of you, from everything with you – and there's no reason you could give me why we shouldn't.'

I stare at him without moving.

'So yeah. That's it. If I could spend another night like last night with you, but with nothing forbidden to us, I think I'd die happy.'

Tears fill my eyes and warm blood rushes to my head.

'In fact, it would really suck to have to die without

getting to do that.' He shrugs. 'I've imagined it so many times it would be a downright tragedy.' He smiles. 'But lucky for you, it's not the end yet for me.'

At 6:10 Ethan is safely back in the car with a chocolate cake in a box, and I am losing my mind.

'Hey, Ethan?'

'Yeah?'

'Could you teach me how to shoot the moon?'

'Right now?' He checks the time on his phone.

'Yes. I promise I'll concentrate.'

He sits up and finds the deck in his duffel bag. 'All right.' He starts dealing cards. 'The time has come.'

I pick up my pile and he picks up his.

'Okay, so you remember the regular strategy of Hearts?'

I nod. 'Pick up no tricks, win no points, and try not to bring attention to yourself,' I say flatly. It's a strategy I am familiar with.

'Well, shooting the moon is the opposite. You can only do it if you have a truly terrible Hearts hand – lots of aces and face cards, preferably most of them hearts. So instead of going for no points, you go for every single point in the game. You try to take every trick and win every point, including the dreaded Queen of Spades.

You go for the whole thing.'

'Got it.' I try to match my enthusiasm to his.

'Of course you have to be sneaky about it. You have to moan and groan and complain about taking each and every heart.'

'I can moan and groan and complain,' I offer.

'Good. And your opponents will be happy to feed you all their hearts until they finally realize what you are trying to do.'

'And then they'll try to stop you?'

'If they can. Hopefully, it'll be too late by then.'

'And if you lose?'

'You mean if you almost shoot the moon? If you get all the points but one or two?'

'Yeah.'

'Well, that's a pretty spectacular loss. You're stuck with, like, twenty-five points. You are through.'

'But if you make it?'

'Pure glory. And you stick every other player with twenty-six points apiece.'

'I like the sound of that.'

'I thought you would.'

'You don't just break some of the rules, you break all of them.'

'Exactly. Fortune favors the bold.'

'Does she?'

Ethan leans toward me and puts his lips on the bare place where my neck curves down into my clavicle. I feel a shiver run down my spine and up my neck into my scalp.

He sits up again. 'I hope so.'

Now it is 6:40. Ethan is outside the car, calling his mother and then his sister, making sure all his lies are holding up. It's nice the way he looks talking to his mom, a lot less guarded than I do.

In a nervous burst of inspiration, I take up my own phone. I find the numbers I'd entered earlier but doubted I would use. My first call is to a home of strangers in Montclair, New Jersey. A message machine picks up, and I pretend to be calling from the office of the county fire inspector. I tell them someone will be stopping by between five o'clock and seven that evening to check that their fire alarms are in working order and make sure they have fire extinguishers on every floor.

'You can look on the county website for the schedule of fines in case our inspector finds any of them to be disabled or faulty,' I say somewhat odiously. I'm not really going to get an inspector over there, but maybe I can scare them into checking their equipment. 'Thank you for participating in fire safety week!' I finish brightly.

The next call is to the police precinct in Ossining. I tell an officer my mother's car has been stolen, and I read out the license plate and description of the car that caused the fatal accident on the Taconic. I give the policewoman the names of the owner's cross streets and say it has last been seen in that area.

'Please call my mother's cell phone if you are able to find it,' I say, and give her a made-up name and number for my mother, using the same last name as the driver just to keep things confusing.

My heart is racing again as I hang up the phone. I feel guilty, imagining the police arriving at the man's house and impounding his car for a night or two, but not that guilty.

Am I breaking rules? Yes. I am crushing them right and left. Am I intervening? You betcha. Am I cheating? Flagrantly. I am throwing elbows into the gut of time. I am lying like a criminal, and it feels both terrible and great.

'Well, here goes,' Ethan murmurs at 7:09 as we get out of the car parked in a lot one building away from the building with the lab. He fumbles with the door locks – up, down, up, down – before he gets them all the way he wants. He's been trying to conceal his nerves, maybe for my benefit, but I can see them now.

We've discussed it, we've rehearsed it, but it all seems a little insufficient now that we're doing it. We're arriving at a murder with a chocolate cake and balloons.

'There's going to be a gun,' I remind him, like he needs reminding.

'I know.'

I shake the balloons. 'Maybe that's what we should be bringing instead of this stuff.'

'Maybe, if either of us had a gun or knew how to shoot a gun, it would,' Ethan says. 'When people like us get guns, you end up with four people dead instead of one.'

He's so endlessly logical, so irritatingly on the mark. 'Okay, fine.'

'We'll be okay, Pren. We've got one huge advantage.'

'What's that?'

'We know what's supposed to happen.'

We hold hands across the parking lot, walking in a slow, expectant trance, as though if we could slow time down, we'd do better at changing it.

I realize we are different now. It's hard to know exactly when it happened, but I picture the kiss on my clavicle having the infectious power of a mosquito bite, transmitting a sweet, exhilarating kind of infection, but weakening all the same. We are no longer able to play two reckless teenagers on the run. We are bound together in a serious way. We have been for a long time, but never like this. Maybe it takes the fragility of our situation to make us see it. It isn't so much having the bond that separates us from our old selves. It is having the bond to lose.

It was easier to think you could sacrifice everything when the old everything was so pale, so lonely compared to this.

It is time to be bold, but as I feel Ethan's sweaty hand sweatily clutching my sweaty hand, I don't feel bold at all. I want to take Ethan back to a safe place, an empty playground, and hold him in my arms until the fateful 51714 is over.

I am again racked with sympathy for people like my mother who don't want to take any risks or fix the future, but just want to live out another day. Maybe it isn't corruption or greed that makes you cowardly. Maybe it's not weakness, suffering, or even fear. Maybe it is love.

I take a long breath. 'Okay.'

'Ready?'

'I'm ready.'

'I'll be close to you all the time. I'm not going to let the guy out of my sight.'

I nod. I'm not sure this makes me feel better.

He kisses me on the temple, another dose, before I go through the glass doors. I cast a last look over my shoulder.

'We'll be fine,' he says. I can't so much hear him as see his lips moving through the glass.

NINETEEN

I'd learned what I could about Mona Ghali's personal life from my research on Ethan's computer. Mona has two sisters, one in Cambridge, Massachusetts, and one in Cairo, Egypt.

Her youngest sister, Maya, recently graduated from Boston University and then moved to Egypt, so she isn't that much older than me.

I arrive on Mona's floor a little after 7:10. The receptionist at the front desk is packing up for the day. I tell her I'm there to see Mona.

'Your name?'

'Uh, Petra.' It's strangely hard to spit it out. 'I'm a friend of her sister's. With a delivery.' I am prepared to say more, but I see the receptionist wants to go home and she doesn't care.

She calls Mona's office and announces me. 'Go ahead back,' the receptionist says, before Mona even responds. 'Two lefts and a right, halfway down the hall.'

It isn't exactly high security. 'It's her birthday,' I say, for no particular reason.

Mona Ghali's name is on a plastic plate to the side of the door, and the door is open. I try to assume a different personality than my regular one as I walk into her office.

'Mona?' I say.

She is sitting at her desk. She looks up from her computer. She has long wavy black hair and large features. When she stands up, she is almost as tall as me.

'I'm Petra Jackson, a friend of Maya's from BU.' I hold out my offerings. 'She asked me to deliver these in person and wish you happy birthday.'

Mona's face is sharp and intelligent. 'Wow. That's really nice. Thanks,' she says, taking them. She lets the balloons float to meet the low ceiling. She peers in the box at the cake. She puts it down on her desk. 'Maya probably told you I'm an insane chocolate addict.'

I nod, silently thanking bold fortune for that.

'My sisters always make such a big deal about birthdays.' Her face is sardonic. 'Were you in her class at school?' Mona asks.

'A year behind. I'm a senior,' I lie.

'Well, thanks for doing this,' she says.

'So listen,' I say, 'is there any way I can talk you into going out and getting a glass of wine or a cup of coffee? My treat. I promised Maya I'd try.'

This is one of the gambits Ethan and I had thought of. On the one hand, it would be safer to get her to a public place and away from the scene of the murder altogether. On the other hand, the earlier and more radically we change the circumstances, the less advantage we have in knowing the future in the first place: What if by getting her out of that building, we only manage to change the venue and the timing of the murder, so we no longer know when and where it will happen?

How tenacious is the future? How tenacious is Andrew Baltos?

Mona rolls her eyes a little. 'So Maya's worried I'm going to spend my birthday alone, is she?'

'No, it's not that. She didn't say that.'

'Well, you can tell her that I'm supposed to be meeting up with someone later.'

Alarms are clanging in my head. That must be Baltos. So it's not a surprise visit – that was one of the things we wondered about.

'Not somebody I'm so particularly eager to see, but contrary to what Maya may think, I'm not just withering alone in my office.'

What does that mean? What is her relationship with him? I look at Mona's expectant face and I realize I need to stay where I am with her, not get ahead. 'I don't think . . .' I begin. My talents at sisterly diplomacy are completely insufficient. 'I'm sure that's not what she meant. I think she just wished she could be here to hang out with you, and so she asked me—'

Mona cuts me off with a gesture. 'Thanks – is it Petra? I appreciate you trying. Maya has the most loyal friends a person could have, but I've actually got to stick around and upload a bunch of things to a new server. Some security breach in our company's system. Like my work is so super secret and in demand.' The sardonic expression is back.

'Maybe it is,' I say earnestly. I probably shouldn't have.

Her computer makes a dinging sound and she goes back to it. 'One set of files done, four more to go.'

I am trying to figure out a way to stay with her that won't sound socially ham-handed or weird. 'Listen,' I say, 'I understand you not wanting to toast your birthday with a total stranger,' I begin.

'You know my sister Maya. You're not a total stranger,' she says.

'Even so, I understand it's kind of an odd offer, and you've got stuff to do. But do you mind if I hang out here for another twenty minutes or so? My friend is coming to pick me up, and he's coming in from the city.'

'That's fine,' she says quickly. 'It's the least I can do after you came all this way. Anyway, it's boring waiting for this stuff to load. This whole lab usually clears out by seven, and it gets kind of creepy here, so I'm happy for the company. Here.' She draws a chair from the corner. 'Sit.' She's not unfriendly, but I don't get the feeling she wants to talk. 'I have another computer you can use if you need to.'

'That's great. Thanks,' I say. I make no move to the computer, but I take a quick look at my phone. 'But if you need to go—'

'This guy I'm meeting up with isn't supposed to be getting here until seven-thirty.'

'Okay,' I say. My pulse is racing. This business is going to unfurl pretty quickly. Hard to imagine how one seemingly ordinary moment in life can stitch to a horrifying, life-ending kind of one.

'How do you like Boston?'

I've never been to Boston. 'I like it a lot.'

'I did too. You're on summer break now?'

'Exactly. Yeah.' My eyes are darting around, waiting

for the next thing to happen. I cast an eye to her filing cabinet. It looks locked, I think. My nerves are coiling.

Part of me wants to keep talking to her, even though I am mostly lying, and part of me just wants us both to shut up and get on with it.

I poke around on my phone and watch her work, until a buzzer rings and I jump as though I never expected that in a million years.

Not so with Mona. She glances casually up from her computer screen. 'That must be him.' She presses a button on her phone, connecting her to an intercom. 'Andrew?'

Don't let him in! Do you know what he's going to do to you? I order my mind to shut up. We need to let this play out.

'Hey, it's me,' I hear a man say.

My heart is pounding in my ears. I try to take normal breaths, to think calmly through the contingencies Ethan and I talked about. *If this happens, then we do that. If this, then that.*

She presses another button, I'm guessing to open the door to the reception area.

I fervently hope Ethan will find a way in through that door behind him. As Mona walks into the hall to meet him, I hang back for a second and push that same button again, just in case.

I can barely bring myself to look at Andrew Baltos walking down the hall. And when I do I am struck by something. He's medium height, stocky, with hair not much longer than stubble on his head mostly covered by a baseball cap. My mind leaps around, trying to make sense of the connection. Lord knows what expressions are running amok on my face.

He looks past Mona to me, and I realize he's studying me carefully too.

Discordantly, I watch Mona greet him with a cool embrace and step aside to make introductions. 'Andrew, this is . . .'

I am fumbly and useless. 'Petra,' I burst out. When assuming a fake name, it's best not to forget it.

'My youngest sister Maya's friend. Petra, this is Andrew.'

He doesn't look so cold-blooded, or so collected himself. He sticks out his hand to shake mine.

Now what? I know what is going to happen, but I can't imagine how it's going to work.

There is something in his eyes. 'Petra?' he repeats. He is trying to figure me out too.

And I realize what it is. His size and shape and the baseball cap on his head remind me in a visceral way of the dark shape I saw running away from my murdered father. Could it be? I couldn't see him well enough to be at all sure, but what if he is?

And if he is, does he recognize me from that night? *This isn't what is supposed to be happening!* If he does, is it going to blow everything? My thoughts are like marbles that fall out of my head and are clacking around on the floor. I wish I could gather them all back.

I picture my father curled like a mealworm on the ground. I try to picture the figure in the baseball cap running away.

I come completely unstuck from the moment. I float off to another place in time. By the time I come back, I've missed the juncture I was watching for. Whatever step I might have had, I lose.

It happens so quickly. They are walking back into her office, and Mona is saying something, possibly to me, that I don't hear. She goes back to her computer to finish the last upload. I am trying to get my excellent eyes to stick on Andrew Baltos, but it's all changing fast. Suddenly he's shoving me toward Mona, and honestly it's as though I never anticipated anything more dramatic than a pleasant conversation.

I fall into her, roughly, trying to regain my balance. He kicks the door shut behind him. Mona is looking up in astonishment, and I follow her eyes to the gun he is pointing at the two of us.

I can't believe this is happening, in spite of everything I know. Why doesn't he care that I am here witnessing his crime? I was supposed to be a deterrent if nothing else, cause some confusion and force him to rethink his plans. Is he going to murder the two of us just as easily as one? Weren't we figuring on some amount of compunction?

Mona opens her mouth, lets out a noise. I put my hand on Mona's arm. I don't know why. I guess it is a gesture of comfort. I am welcoming her to her destiny.

And as I am trying to collect my marbles, I wonder, *How am I going to stop this?*

'Go over there,' Baltos says, gesturing with the gun. 'Sit down against the wall.'

Mona looks at him in disbelief. Her eyes simply didn't comprehend it enough to be afraid. 'Are you serious? What is going on?'

'Go!'

I pull her by the arm to the wall. I sit her down. I comprehend it plenty well to be afraid. A part of me just wants it to be over with. I don't want Ethan to arrive at all.

Andrew Baltos keeps the gun pointed at us and steps

over to her computer. I see the sweat soaking in big U shapes under his arms, patches down his back. With his other hand he navigates her screen. Within minutes of searching, his frustration quickly blooms. 'What did you do?' he demands of Mona. He walks toward us. 'Where are the EFP studies?'

I can see suspicion dawning on Mona's face. 'I moved them.'

'Where?'

'Someplace safe,' she says.

He goes to the other computer, a laptop, and searches its hard drive quickly, keeping the gun trained on us. He grows impatient with it and shoves it away.

He stands up and goes to the filing cabinet. I pray it is locked. He pulls at each of the drawers, cursing. With one arm he throws the heavy cabinet to the ground. It catches the side of the desk chair and flips the chair up on its side. Two of the file drawers pop open, and papers and folders spill out.

There is chaos of noise. Baltos has his back to the door and is leaning over to pick up files, and Ethan takes this moment to enter the office. I draw in a sharp breath as Ethan drives his shoulder into Baltos's back.

Mona screams and I clutch her hand. Baltos smashes into the desk, and Ethan violently strips the hand holding the gun. The gun slides across the carpet toward Mona and me, and I reach for it. I think of what Ethan said about us and guns, but what am I going to do? I stand and point it shakily at Baltos. 'Stand up,' I say. I can't quite believe myself.

Baltos more or less complies, slowly getting up from where he'd collided with the desk. Ethan steps away from him.

Mona is staring, mystified, at Ethan. 'What are you doing here?'

'Stand up,' I order Andrew Baltos again. 'Put your hands out.' I use my second hand to steady my first on the gun. I glance at Ethan. I test the feel of the trigger against my index finger.

Ethan comes close to me. I can feel he wants to reach for me but doesn't. He doesn't risk interfering with my concentration. 'Are you okay?' he asks under his breath.

'Yes,' I say. I want to look at him, for him to prop me up, and I also want to cry, but I don't dare take my eyes off Baltos.

'Is Ethan the friend you were waiting for?' Mona asks. I nod.

Ethan approaches Baltos again. 'Keep your arms out in front of you,' he tells him. He takes the wallet from Baltos's back pocket. 'Now reach your arms up,' Ethan says. He reaches into Baltos's shirt pocket and takes out his phone.

Ethan steps back and I can't help but look at his face. There's something in his expression that spooks me. 'What is it?' I ask him.

He shakes his head.

'Ethan, tell me.'

'The gorilla.'

'What?'

'He's a traveler,' Ethan says to me under his breath.

'Can't be.'

'He is.'

'He can't be.'

'I can see it very clearly.'

My hands are shaking horribly. 'He's in the newspaper.'

Mona and Baltos are staring at us. Nobody is moving.

'I think he's your Moses,' Ethan says quietly.

♦ TWENTY

Everything that happens after that is my fault. I am trying to make sense of what Ethan is saying and I lose my focus. I lose my nerve.

Where is he from? He didn't come with us. What does it mean? The newspaper was written seventy years before we came.

When Baltos slams Ethan with his fist in the side of the head, I don't shoot Baltos as I should. For that split second my eyes follow Ethan.

Baltos takes the moment to charge into me at full force. He throws me backward. My head hits the wall. I don't even know what happens with the gun.

Mona cries out. I struggle to stay conscious and alert. I have to protect Ethan. I crawl across the floor to reach him, but Baltos is up on his feet, his gun back in his hand.

Baltos is rattled too. His hand is unsteady. 'Why are you making this so difficult?' he demands. 'All three of you. Put your backs against that wall.'

We do as he says. Ethan has his hands on me, checking to see that I'm all right. I hear Mona crying.

He gestures to me and Ethan. 'I don't want anything to do with you. Why are you here?' His voice nearly cracks with the strain of it.

'We're not going to stand back and let you kill her,' Ethan says.

Baltos shakes his head. He looks like he's going to be sick. 'You don't get to decide.'

Ethan is pushing himself up from sitting. Now it's me clutching at him, trying to pull him down.

Baltos turns on him. 'Just stay where you are, all right?' he explodes. 'If you move, I'll shoot you.' He is agitated. He looks crazy. He is Moses. He is Traveler One. But he doesn't save us. He destroys us.

Ethan shakes free of my hand and gets up. 'Ethan, stop!' I scream. I can hear myself sobbing. This is how it happens. I can't let it happen.

Suddenly the gun is less than half a foot from Ethan's head. I hear the barrel click. 'Please, no,' I cry. I tackle Ethan to the floor and in that moment, Baltos turns and fires the gun directly into Mona Ghali's chest.

In horror I watch as her chest seems to cave and then open. I scream again.

Baltos's body is shaking. He drops the gun on the ground. He looks almost as horrified as we do, like he wasn't expecting this, this wet and warm and living horror to be the result of pulling a dry trigger on a gun. He throws the door open and disappears down the hall.

Gazing at Mona, angled wrong and open-eyed on the floor, I hear the heavy, rushed footsteps getting fainter.

'She's dead,' Ethan says, and I know that's true. He picks the gun up off the floor. Before I can do anything to stop him, he is gone.

I get up and go after him. I don't know what else to do.

How long does thinking take? Does it fit into time? I think it is strange that the whole world can change in the time it takes to run across a dark parking lot.

At one end of the parking lot I am still fighting the natural order of time, still hoping to defy her. I am failing, but I am fighting. I lost Mona, but I am not letting her get Ethan.

At the other end of the parking lot, I know it is something else. I am not fighting time. She's not really my enemy. I am fighting Andrew Baltos, Traveler One. He is the one who did this to her, to us. Mighty fate is injured and confused, like Babar's mother after the hunters get her, and I am trying to help undo a terrible injustice. I am trying to give the poor soul a break.

I hear a gunshot.

My whole body turns icy. I am running on these terrible icy limbs of mine, though I can barely feel them. I am crying warmly, melting my own icy face.

You better not have, I say in my mind to Andrew Baltos. *You just better not have.*

I can't see either of them anymore. The sound of the shot came from the wooded area beyond the parking lot. I run, icily, to where I heard the sound.

A few yards out I see two dark figures, one standing and the other on the ground. I sprint wildly toward the figure on the ground, ready to throw my arms around my beloved, but when I get there, I pull up short. It's Andrew Baltos on the ground. Beloved son, brother, and friend is standing up and holding the gun, as alive as I am.

My whole body is flooding with warmth. 'What happened? Is he dead?' I look down and I see he's not. He's writhing, though.

'I shot him in the leg,' Ethan says. His voice is flat. He hasn't gotten around to feeling all this yet. Calmly, he takes a phone out of his pocket, the one he took from Baltos. I watch him, for the second time in four days, call 911. 'My name is Andrew Baltos,' he says into the phone. 'I'm at 7736 River Road, Teaneck. Sixth floor. I just shot someone. I believe she is dead.' He ends the call.

I can't calm down, not any part of myself. But my limbs are thawing in all this warm relief. 'Is he okay? What are you going to do about him?' I say, looking down on him. He's a poor specimen, our Moses.

'I'm going to call an ambulance and stay until it gets here. But before I do, we're going to talk to him.'

Andrew Baltos is writhing, but I sense he is also listening.

'If he talks too slow, he might bleed to death, but otherwise he ought to be fine,' Ethan says, amply loud so he will hear.

I look at Ethan's hands. In the darkness a phone is glinting in one fist and a gun in the other. I reach out and take the gun from him. I wind up and throw it. The three of us watch it spinning through the air. I've never thrown anything farther in my life. I hope the muddy ground is muddy enough to swallow it up forever.

'Why did you do that?' Ethan says. He's more surprised than mad, I think.

'No more shooting today,' I say. For the first time, I let

myself tug at the corner of the thought that Ethan will
be okay.

'Who are you?'

At first Andrew Baltos is not in the mood to talk. But
over a couple of minutes it seems to dawn on him that
he's not in the mood to bleed to death either.

'What do you mean, who am I?' he grunts. 'I am the
guy you just shot in the leg.'

Within a couple of minutes we are listening to the
first siren. And then to a lot of sirens.

Ethan is all business. 'I know you are a traveler.'

This stops the writhing.

'I want to know when you came from. Why
you came.'

The man is in pain and he's mad and he's flabbergasted,
and Ethan sure did get his attention. 'How do you
know this?'

'I can see it from looking at you. I've never seen a
traveller who's less assimilated.'

'And you've seen others?' Baltos sounds sarcastic.

'I have.' He points to me. 'Her, for example.'

Andrew Baltos sits up and tucks his leg under him
protectively. His face is pale, looking from one of us to
the other. 'Why should I believe this?'

'Up to you,' says Ethan. 'It will save time if you do. I want to know why you came. Why you murdered Mona Ghali.'

'Because she destroyed the lives of good people, including my father. Because I am making the world a better place.'

This is so extraordinary I almost fall over. There's hint of irony in his voice, but a lot of sincerity too. It's hard to listen to it, picturing Mona's body torn apart on the floor of her office.

'She's a pivotal person, you know. Was. Will be. Would have been.' He coughs at the range of tenses. 'She became chief engineer at my father's energy company, and she turned around and gutted the place. She got the government regulators in there to tear it apart. She destroyed the company he built and put four and a half thousand of his good people out of work. My father hanged himself by his necktie in his office when he was fifty-five years old.'

I can see the pain raw in his face. I feel the force driving his mission, horrible as it is.

'And it doesn't stop with that. The work she's doing now destroys not just companies but entire industries in a matter of a few years: oil, gas, coal, the refineries, pipelines, tar shale and tar sands extraction, hydraulic fracturing. Do you know how many lives depend on those?'

Watching him talk, I see that his eyes are alight, as though he didn't just leave a woman dead in an office building a quarter of a mile away. I wonder if maybe the experiences he finds here aren't quite real to him. Like the Monopoly-money version of life, where it doesn't really matter how you spend it.

'I met her when she was old, and by then she was a monster. Putting millions of people out of jobs, destroying the lifeblood of whole countries. Even her own people, the Egyptians. Not even a care. I am sorry to kill a young woman. Truly, I don't like to do it. But it serves the greater good.'

I can hear the cadence in his voice that is familiar to me and different from most people here. The softening of the 'th' sound. He wasn't trained out of it like we were. Sickening to recognize, he is one of us but not from the same place. He is talking about the future, I realize, but a different future from mine.

'So you came back here to kill her?' Ethan asks evenly. 'That's why you came back?'

'I am not the only one who wanted it.'

'Did others come with you?'

'No. I'm here alone.'

Ethan squats down so he can look the man in the eye. 'I want to tell you a story I learned recently from a man, a dear friend of mine. Are you ready to listen?'

He grimaces like he's not so ready to listen, but what choice does he have?

'Sixty years from now, a sick, crazy old man is living in an institution not far from here,' Ethan begins. 'He writes to my friend and begs him to come visit before he dies. My friend does and finds a raving, ranting lunatic trying to scratch out his own eyeballs. Nobody has listened to a word this man has said in twenty-five years, though he was once a hugely successful businessman. But my friend does listen, and this poor man pieces together an extraordinary story. He tells my friend he is a time traveler. His mind is gone – he's lost all the dates and the places and names but one. He remembers this day: May 17, 2014. In fact, he is terrified he will forget it. He carves it on the walls, into the floor. He cuts it savagely into his own skin. He is haunted by this date, this number, because he says it was the day he destroyed the world. He said he did many thoughtless and reckless things in his travels, and he regrets all of them, but what he did on this day, he now understands was the critical stroke. And my friend understands that this man is sick in his heart and his head because of what he has done.

Crazy as he is, the old man sees the crisis of the climate spreading, the disintegrating ice sheets and food shortages and massive starvation and anarchy. He recognizes there is no coming back from it. And he's right, by the way, except that it's far worse than he even knows. The blood plagues don't sweep the world until several years after he is dead. He's the only one who knows that the future he abandoned was a robust place compared to what he sees around him. Only he can compare the two, and he knows he is responsible for the devastation. There's one thing this man says to my friend again and again. "Don't let me do it. Please, help me. Kill me if you have to. Just don't let me do it.'"

Ethan stands up. He rubs his hands together. 'You know, of course, that the sick, raving, self-mutilating bastard is you.'

♦ TWENTY-ONE

We go to the police station to give statements that night. We keep it simple: Ethan's an intern at the lab and a friend of Mona's. We brought gifts for her birthday and got caught in the middle of the deadly shooting. Crime of passion? Well, maybe so. Ethan retrieved the gun, chased him down, and so on. I confess to throwing the gun. Ethan helps me draw a map so they can locate it. I explain I didn't want any more killing. Needless to say, we leave out the stories about raving time travelers who destroy the planet.

It's late and we want to leave. The officers on duty look pretty eager to wrap it up themselves. They make an appointment for us to give more detailed statements to a detective the following afternoon.

I am ready to burst by the time we get out of there.

'That story you told Andrew Baltos. Did my father really tell you that?' I ask as we walk from the station to Ethan's car.

'No,' he says.

I stop. 'What?'

'He told me a few pieces of it, you filled in some others, a bit of it I made up. But I didn't put it all together until tonight in the woods when Baltos told us why he had done it. I didn't know Baltos was a traveler until I got to the lab tonight, and it was all unfolding. I wish I had. Maybe then we could have succeeded rather than failed.'

We walk past his car and keep going. I guess we both need to keep moving under the open sky for a while. We walk along dark empty sidewalks in silence, holding hands. It's hard to absorb everything we've been through.

I realize I just want to hold his hand until midnight comes to end this day. And that's what we do. We end up finding another deserted playground and sitting on the top bars of a jungle gym when midnight passes. The clouds are thick. We can see the moon only sporadically.

'Even though we knew, and even though we tried to stop it, it all happened anyway, just like the newspaper said.' Ethan sounds tired and defeated.

'That's not true. Not all of it,' I say.

'Maybe the details are different. But the stuff that matters is the same.'

I shake my head. 'That's not true either.' I tap my feet against the metal bar, wondering how to say it. 'The newspaper said you were supposed to die.'

He just looks at me. He doesn't say anything.

I take in two big lungfuls of air and let them out. I feel like every muscle in my body is knotted. 'I discovered it early this morning, and I've been agonizing over it since.' I take the page folded up small out of my pocket and hand it to him. 'I feel guilty, because I didn't really come here tonight wanting to protect Mona Ghali. I wanted to protect you.'

He studies it carefully, trying to make out the small words in the dim light cast by a playground lamp. 'Holy shit.' Finally he nods. 'Well, I'm glad that didn't happen.'

I actually laugh. It sounds sort of like a laugh, anyway. 'Yeah, me too.'

'I'm glad you didn't tell me.'

'Are you? I wasn't sure.'

'Yes, I am. However, if I was dead, I might feel differently.'

Out of my mouth comes that laughlike sound again.

He's quiet for a minute. 'So when you asked me

what I wanted to do before I died, you weren't kidding around?'

I shake my head.

'And still you didn't give me what I wanted?' His outrage is a bit overdone.

I shake my head repentantly. 'There weren't a lot of opportunities today, if you think back on it. Besides, I wasn't going to let you die. It would have been a freebie.'

He laughs. 'I like freebies.'

We fall into silence.

'You know what else is good?' I say.

'What?'

'He didn't get her research. I watched her upload everything onto that server you gave her. You have it now.'

Ethan's eyes open a bit wide. 'That's true. That's very good. God, that's a big responsibility. I'm going to go home and upload it to a dozen different places. I'm even going to print it all out on honest-to-God paper.'

'Ben Kenobi would be proud.'

Ethan looks happy with that.

'You know what else is good?' I say.

He smiles at me now. 'What?'

'He didn't escape the country with some fake passport. He's in the hospital and soon will be in police custody.'

'Yes. I thought of that too. That is also very good.'

The moon comes out from behind a cloud. It looks so close tonight. It gives us each a shadow on the pavement below.

'How do you think it would have happened? I mean, without you here or your father?'

'I've been thinking about that,' I say. 'You were probably at the lab for some reason.' I shrug. 'Without me, you'd have more time on your hands.'

'True. And I'd need someone else to help me with my physics problems.'

I snort. 'Right.' I stretch out my fingers, studying their long shadows beneath us. 'So you tried to help Mona Ghali, just like tonight. You somehow got in the way. Maybe you were just walking by and a bullet came through the window. Maybe you weren't even in the building. Maybe Baltos was rushed and flustered, pulling out in his car after it happened, and he hit you a block away and never stopped. God, I don't know.'

He is nodding. 'All possible.'

'You know what I think?' I ask.

'What?'

'I think we broke it open. I really do. We've officially opened the gap between what the newspaper says and what is true. I think we're going to get a new future now.

It may not be perfect. It may even be worse. Though it's hard to see how it could be worse with you in it. But I don't need to read the newspaper tomorrow to know that the reality is going to be different.'

Ethan puts his arm around my shoulders, and our two shadows become one nice blob. 'Maybe we'll find a traveler from this future who can tell us how it is,' he says.

I look at the sky wistfully, hoping not. 'Maybe nobody knows,' I say.

We find an all-night diner in Tenafly and pick at eggs and toast under a harsh light. I think of Ethan's all-he-could-eat buffet that morning. It's been a really long day.

It's tough to fathom doing much in the way of sleeping, between the night we've had and the morning we are planning. We end up parking in the lot of a Best Buy. We hold on to each other in the backseat like we're the only two people left.

'Hey, Ethan?' How I love saying his name.

'Yeah.'

'I feel bad not giving you the thing you said you wanted if you knew you were going to die.'

He laughs and holds me a little tighter. 'As you should.'

'So even though you're not going to die, I think maybe we should do it anyway. Do you?'

He laughs again. 'Seriously?'

'Yeah. I think you are right about the lies. I think the leaders just want to keep us away from happiness.'

'Those are words straight to my heart, Henny.'

'I mean, I'm not saying we should do it now. Not, like, this minute. It wouldn't be right. But soon. We both need to go home and get our lives sorted out. But maybe Friday?' I know this is wishful thinking. I don't know what kind of life I'm going back to, but I don't care. I need something to hold on to. 'We could meet somewhere remote and beautiful.'

'Haverstraw Creek?'

'Maybe. Yes. I'll bring a picnic.'

'Can we camp out all night?' He sounds excited. 'I'll bring a tent and two sleeping bags.' He pauses. 'Maybe one sleeping bag.'

'I don't know about all night, but some of it. We'll see.'

He puts his head back down on the seat. He snuggles in a little closer. 'How am I going to make it until Friday?' he asks before he falls asleep.

I feel his body against mine, the little twitches as he goes over to sleep. It's a matter of great trust, I think, to be able to fall asleep in a person's arms.

I smell the cloth upholstery under my head. I can't say the car is all that comfortable, and it's certainly not beautiful, but of all the places I've ever slept in my life, the back of Ethan's neighbor's car with Ethan is my favorite one.

I call my mother in the early morning and ask her to meet us at Mr. Robert's office at nine. It's going to be a doozy.

I tell her I'm okay. I hope she's okay. I don't want to talk more than that.

On the way we pick up a newspaper. The New York Times dated Sunday, May 18, 2014. 'Don't we already have one of those?' Ethan jokes.

We pass it back and forth a couple of times. Neither of us wants to look at it.

Why? I don't know. Ethan folds it up and puts it in his duffel bag. It seems to me it would be like reading the detailed autopsy report for someone you knew. It's important that it's there, maybe, in case you need it. But you don't want to read it.

◆ TWENTY-TWO

We knock on the door of Mr. Robert's office at nine sharp. My mom is already there. I can't describe the looks we get walking in.

I introduce Ethan to my mom, though she's met him before. She looks as though she's been crying.

'I'm sorry, Molly,' I say in a low voice to her. 'I'm sorry for putting you through all this.'

'And this is Mr. Robert,' I say to Ethan. Honestly, Mr. Robert looks like he is in the process of swallowing his tongue.

'Robert. Just Robert,' he mutters. His throat is expanding like a bullfrog's. He tugs at his collar. 'It's good to meet you, uh, Ethan,' he says. 'And now I'd like to ask you to leave and let us talk to Prenna privately.'

'I'd like to stay,' Ethan says. He doesn't sound

threatening or bratty. He sounds immovable.

Mr. Robert is staring deadly eye beams at me. 'Prenna.' He clears his throat. 'I think the people who care most about you, like your mother and your friend Katherine Wand, would really appreciate it if you would be reasonable and speak to us *privately*.'

I glance at my mother. I can't read her face. At least she appears to be unharmed.

'You've really made life *difficult* for them, and you'll only make it worse,' he adds, sympathetic as can be.

I am not putting up with his bullshit. For one thing, it just takes too long. 'Let's sit down,' I say, and Ethan and I do. 'We are going to talk openly and honestly, the four of us, and it's going to make you very uncomfortable. But hopefully, you'll get used to it.'

'Prenna.' It's that warning tone I have gotten from Mr. Robert roughly one million times.

'Let's start with this,' I say. 'Ethan knows who we are. No use keeping secrets at this point.'

'*Prenna*.' More tongue swallowing from Mr. Robert. 'You certainly want *to be careful*,' he hisses.

I look at him. 'No, I don't.'

'Prenna, are you sure—' My mother looks desperately ill at ease.

'Ethan doesn't know about us because I told him,'

I continue. 'Ethan knows because he was there at the river in April 2010 when we arrived here. He saw the strange atmosphere at the end of the time path. He saw me, though I have no memory of it. He gave me the New York Giants sweatshirt. Remember? That you gave me such a hard time about?'

I stare at Mr. Robert. 'Won't you sit down?' I pick up the bowl of jelly beans from the table. 'Jelly bean?'

Neither of them says anything. I was sort of counting on this. Once I get going, Mr. Robert won't want to risk saying anything in front of Ethan that might make it sound like he is accepting my premise. Any premise. And my mother will follow his lead. I think this is good because it will speed things up.

'But that's not what I'm here to talk about,' I say. At last Mr. Robert sits in his interrogation chair and my mother follows, sitting around the corner of the sectional sofa. 'I am here to tell you, Mr. Robert, that you have to leave me alone. You must let Katherine come home and leave her alone. You must leave my mother alone. Even if they don't demand it, I do.'

'Really. Is that so?' he sputters, red faced.

'Yes, it is. I'm not afraid of you, and I'm not afraid of the rules. At least, I'm not afraid of breaking the rules that matter. The future you are clinging to – the place we came from – wasn't created by the regular order of things. It was created by a traveler – the famous Traveler One. He does exist. We've met him. And he may or may not have handed down our rules, but if he did, it was only after he broke every single one of them.'

Silence. My mother's face has opened in surprise.

'Ethan and I aren't trying to disrupt the sequence of time; we're trying to fix it.'

'Prenna, how do you know this?'

Mr. Robert glares at my mother for this, but I am so relieved.

'A man named Andrew Baltos arrived here from an earlier point in the future. I don't know exactly when or how, but I am certain of it. I also know his version of the future was different and a lot less dire than ours, and I believe the difference comes from the things he has done while he's been here.'

Mr. Robert looks truly astonished. I wonder if he or the other counselors know any of this.

I try as simply and as clearly as I can to summarize everything that happened on May 17, 2014. I talk mostly to my mother, because I can feel that she is listening.

'It's the right thing to protect time's natural sequence,' I say to them, to her. 'We were right to try. But now that we know it's been twisted and mistreated by a traveler like us, I think it's right to try to fix it and contain the damage. We didn't save Mona, but we saved her research and we've stopped Baltos, at least for the time.' I glance at Ethan. I don't tell them about Ethan, and I leave Poppy's part out too. It just seems too much for now. 'I think we did enough to open things up. I think we're on a different course. At least, I really hope we are. Even you have to agree, Mr. Robert, there's no point in propping up a future that's an absolute trauma, if we're honest about it. We might as well just let go of it and work for a better one, you know?'

I look at Mr. Robert. I don't think he knows.

'I'm not saying we should tell people where we come from. I'm happy to keep that secret, if you prefer. We create a lot less impact that way. But you should know I am not scared to let it out if you force it. Do you understand what I'm saying?'

I am not expecting a nod or anything.

'I think it's time for us to assimilate for real, to let go of the surveillance and the intimidation you call counseling and the punishments. Let's get rid of the glasses and the pills. You're not helping us, you're hurting us, Mr. Robert. You know it's true.'

I turn to my mother. 'I stopped taking the pills and my eyes are perfect. I don't need the glasses anymore, and you must know the glasses are for watching us.'

I study her face, her eyes cast down. Did she know about the pills? Didn't she know about the pills? In my heart I don't think she knew. I'm not quite done with this topic.

'Molly, you need to figure out what's in those pills, if you don't already know. If there's anything good in them, you need to separate it from the poison that is blinding us.'

She lifts her eyes to me, and I now see that she is desperate to talk. I can see she has questions. Her eyes are alive in a way I haven't seen in a long time. But she won't talk here.

'Let's try to contain the damage done by Andrew Baltos as best we can,' I carry on, 'and beyond that live as good citizens and good family members and see where things go. That's what I think we should do.'

I look up again. Silence.

'I know, I know, Mr. Robert. You've got big plans for me. You're planning to take me from my bed tonight, if not sooner, and put a quick end to me. You'd do that to me for just a fraction of the things I've done.'

My mother looks horrified, though of course she knows it's true. 'Prenna—'

'It's okay,' I say to her. 'They're not going to do that.

They are going to leave me alone.' I turn to Mr. Robert and fix my gaze on him. 'Here is why.' I stop and look around, trying to guess where the cameras might be. 'I'm pretty sure Mrs. Crew and the rest of the leaders are watching this meeting, but in case they aren't, I want you to share it with them as soon as possible. Nobody besides Ethan knows anything about us now. And Ethan can be trusted to keep our secret. He's done it for four years already. But if you do anything more to harm me or my mother or Katherine, it won't stay that way. I will go to the Immigration and Naturalization Service first. They will want to get our immigration status squared away, and that is going to be interesting, to say the least. After that I'll go to the IRS, I'll go to Child Protective Services, and finally, if I need to, I'll go to the police. Aside from just the minor stuff – the drugging, kidnapping, and illegal surveillance – you've done some other things that law enforcement might see as even more problematic.' I do kind of hope Mrs. Crew is watching. 'And thanks to you, it's all recorded.'

I look at Ethan and he smiles a small smile at me. I must say, I am sort of enjoying myself. I love the truth. I really do. And I really hate Mr. Robert.

So why stop here? "Mr. Robert, you are probably thinking, 'No, she's not. We'll never give her the chance.

I'd kill her right this second if I didn't have to wait for Ethan and her mother to get out of the room.' But you are wrong. If you put me away, Ethan will use the huge amount of information we have compiled and do it for me. My disappearance will be one more piece of damning evidence. And Ethan is smart. He knows everything about us. He's a good programmer and a devilish hacker. He's already uploaded files to a whole network of servers. If you mess with him, he's made sure the information we've got will immediately be distributed to every agency I mentioned along with a whole bunch of carefully chosen news shows and media outfits. I know it will be a fascinating story. Seriously, we will dominate the news cycle for months on end.' Now I should stop. I'm being reckless, but I can't seem to hold back. 'If you choose that, be sure to whiten those teeth and lose a few pounds, Mr. Robert, because the camera really does put on weight. And no offense, but that's the last thing you need.'

I need to shut up. I think we are almost done. 'So we could do all that. Or, as I suggested, we could live as good citizens – quiet, law-abiding normal citizens – and see where things go. Your choice.'

Nothing. Silence. I'm having trouble reading even my mother's face at this point.

'You don't need to tell me anything right now,' I offer.

'You can talk it over with the leaders, and then you can show me. If you and the leaders agree to my suggestions, then I want to see my friend Katherine Wand at my house by five o'clock tomorrow evening. No boarding school, no matter how terrific, can be farther away than that. If I see her, I'll figure we've got a deal. If not, I'll get started with the INS. Or, I guess, Ethan can get started on my behalf if something happens to me. Or, I guess, one of Ethan's numerous proxies will get started on our behalf if anything should happen to him.'

I stand and walk toward Mr. Robert. I pull up close to him so I can be sure he sees and understands exactly what I mean. 'I am not afraid to blow it open, Mr. Robert. I have nothing to lose. I will not hesitate if you give me a reason. But I'd rather not. I'd rather we live in peace and quiet and make the best of the new future that's unfolding. I will be agreeable if you will. But no more threats, no more punishments, no more surveillance.' I fix him with a good long look. 'That is over.'

TWENTY-THREE

It's a busy kind of a day.

Ethan checks home with his mom, sets up a few things on his home computer, and returns the neighbor's car. Seniors are done with classes, but he needs to go by school to take care of a couple of things. We promised to be back in Teaneck by one in the afternoon to give full statements about the murder. After that we drive to the storage place in the Bronx and don't arrive at Holy Cross Medical Center in Teaneck until almost six o'clock.

I bring the last three months of my old memory bank, a copy of my unfinished essay on the first blood plague, and a couple of the letters I wrote to my brother in a sealed envelope. I want Andrew Baltos to know how it really was. I'm not sure if he'll be able to read the memory bank, but I suspect he'll figure something out. Maybe

270

he'll never get out of prison. But maybe he will and it will somehow make a difference.

We've had to get permission from the detective for our visit to Baltos, and of course we agreed to the presence of the armed guard they have stationed at the door of his hospital room.

It's strange, because when we get to his hospital room, Baltos doesn't seem unhappy to see us. His leg is all bound up and he looks reasonably healthy. He greets us almost as though we are friends. 'Good of you to visit,' he says, and it doesn't sound purely sarcastic.

He turns his gaze to Ethan. 'Who are you? It's been driving me crazy all last night and today. Even when I'm sleeping, it's like pins in my brain. I know you.'

Ethan shakes his head. 'I don't think so. If I'd met you, I would remember.'

'No, no. I don't mean in this time. Later. Much later. In the sixties. You are much older, but I am sure I know you.'

Ethan raises his eyebrows. 'Well, then I wouldn't remember, would I?'

'Tell me your name. Maybe that will help.'

'Ethan Jarves. Born in January 1996.'

'Oh, shit. Really?'

'Yes.'

271

'Of course. The scientist.'

'I don't know. Am I?'

'Sure. You worked with Mona, but you weren't like her. You were a hero of mine. I always wanted to find you here.' His eyes are bright. Almost too bright. I think that in his opinion Ethan has gone from Monopoly money to the real thing.

My eyes are bright too. I relish this version of the future with beloved Ethan in it. I am more and more compelled by the possibility that the critical person lost at the fork on May 17 was not Mona, but Ethan.

'You're the expert on this stuff. In fact,' Baltos goes on, "I was thinking you could help me find my way back.' He laughs a strange laugh. 'I've got a girl back home, my first love, and I miss her like crazy.' He looks like he's kidding, but only partly.

'I don't know,' Ethan says. 'I'm not a scientist yet. I'm only eighteen.'

He's nodding slowly. I realize there are tears in his eyes. 'I'm not going to get back, am I?' He looks from Ethan to me and back to Ethan.

It's a serious question, and I realize somewhat bitterly that the future he comes from has got to be a whole hell of a lot better than mine was if he's wishing he could go back to it.

'I don't think so,' Ethan says.

'Yeah, no.' He sighs a long sigh. 'Well, you're the man, you know that? You're the expert on this stuff. You are a brilliant kid. It's a good thing I didn't kill you yesterday.'

I squeeze Ethan's hand hard. I press my lips together so I don't make a sound.

Ethan is remarkably calm. 'Yeah, I was glad about that too.'

I take a breath and steady myself. 'Mr. Baltos, I need to ask you about something else.'

'Let's hear it.'

'Who is Theresa Hunt?'

'Old girlfriend of mine.'

'And Jason Hunt?'

He looks less comfortable. 'Her kid. My kid too, according to her.'

'Allan Cotes?'

'That's the guy she married a couple of years ago. He's bringing up Jason.'

'Do you know where Theresa is now?'

'No. I haven't spoken with her in at least a year.'

'What about Josie Lopez?'

'Wow, what is this?' Baltos narrows his eyes at me. 'She's another former girlfriend. Why are you asking?'

'These are all people who've been hospitalized with a

mysterious virus. I think it must have something to do with you.'

'God. Is that true?' His surprise looks genuine. 'Are you sure about that?'

'Pretty sure.'

He shakes his head. 'I'm not sick. I haven't been sick – not seriously – since I got here. I don't have any mysterious virus, I'm sure of that.'

I try to think of the right question to ask. 'What year did you leave to come here?'

He raises an eyebrow at me. 'It was April of 2068. I haven't told anybody here where I come from. Besides the two of you, nobody knows.'

'That's probably a good thing,' I say. 'So when you left, were there any major disease outbreaks or plagues?' I ask. 'Have you heard of the blood plague? They also called it Dama Virus X?'

He considers. 'I never heard of that. There were some avian flus and that kind of thing. AIDS was done with by that point. Nothing really big stands out.'

'Okay,' I say. 'That's all. Thanks.' I look to Ethan. 'We should go.' I hand Baltos the envelope we brought. 'When you get a chance, look through it. I want you to see how different things got after you came here.'

Andrew Baltos leans back to rest his head. He looks

puzzled, a bit apprehensive, but not completely resistant. 'You brought things back with you?'

'My dad did.'

'All right. I'll take a look.'

We're at the door when Baltos clears his throat. We both turn. 'I said I was glad I didn't shoot you yesterday, Ethan, but now that I think of it, maybe I wish I had.'

I am hoping he isn't getting any ideas. 'Why?'

'If it weren't for Ethan, I wouldn't be here. I'd be back home with my first girl. Yesterday never would have happened. None of this would ever have happened.'

Ethan looks a little wary. 'And why is that?'

'Because you are the reason I'm here. You told me about the day you went fishing when you were a kid. You even showed me a picture. That's how I knew where to come.'

When I finally get to my house, it is late and dark. Ethan wants to come in with me, but I talk him out of it. I don't want to push my mother too far.

I put my key in the lock and half expect a replay of the last time I went home. I step into the hall, but my mom's worried face is not bearing down on me this time. I glance at the dining room but see no sign of the detested duo. I check all the other rooms in the house just to be sure. I am ready for an ambush, but nothing comes. My mother's not even home.

I go to the front of the house and flick on some lights. I wave to Ethan from the dining room window as I promised to let him know the coast is clear. He pauses for another few seconds before he drives off. I think it's hard for him to leave. I know it's hard to be left.

I turn on the light in the kitchen, and I see a note and a box of Mallomars on the counter. My heart lifts. I love Mallomars. I know my mom must be telling me something with those.

Prenna,

Out at a meeting tonight. Lots to talk about. Enjoy the cookies, sleep well, and I'll see you in the morning.

Love,
Molly/Mom

I do enjoy the cookies. I enjoy five of them while sitting on the kitchen counter. Then I drink a glass of milk. I lose myself in those pleasures. I can't think of anything else today.

I crawl into my bed. I have never been so tired in my

life. I hope I don't wake up to find myself in the back of Mr. Douglas's car or tied up in the basement of that farm. I'm so tired I might not notice.

I see a text from Ethan.

Is it Friday yet?

TWENTY-FOUR

I don't wake up in the basement of the farm. I wake up in my warm bed at nine-forty-five with the sun blasting through my window. I wake up to the smell of bacon and . . . something. Pancakes. Could it be?

I feel like I've woken in my own bed, but in a different family. I don't think my mother has ever made breakfast since we've lived here.

In wonder, I watch the woman bustling around the kitchen. Not only are there pancakes, but they have blueberries in them. She's set two places at the table with place mats and cloth napkins and the works. Like a real family.

'This is amazing,' I say to her when we've sat down. 'Thank you.'

She looks at me over her coffee cup. I watch her

remove her glasses and close them in the drawer of the sideboard. 'I feel like the world is waking up again.'

It may be the most hopeful thing I've ever heard her say. Her plain eyes are beautiful, though I don't think she can see much out of them yet.

There is indeed a lot to talk about, and I feel that between us. The first subject is the hardest one. I hate to unleash a cloud over pancakes, but it can't be helped.

'I know it was Poppy.'

Her coffee cup goes down. Her guard starts to go up.

'I know it's easier not to think so, but it was.'

She takes a while with this. I see her hands are shaky with her fork and knife. 'Why do you think he stayed away?'

'I think he was trying to protect us for as long as he could. He needed to follow his mission without feeling like he was bringing danger on anybody but himself.'

She stops trying to eat or even focus her eyes. She looks lost.

'He's the one we have to thank for everything. He knew about the fork on May seventeenth. He compiled the material to figure it out and he staked everything to make sure it didn't pass without us doing something.'

She nods tentatively.

'He brought back some unbelievable stuff with him.

He left it in a storage unit in the Bronx, and when you are ready I will take you. There is our family memorabilia, our memory banks and many thousands of dollars in cash, a lot of it dated in the future.'

My mother looks stricken, officially overwhelmed. It's going to take a while for this to sink in.

'And a bunch of future newspapers.' I picture the pile. 'All now inaccurate, I hope. Maybe you can help me figure out what to do with it.' I take a sip of orange juice.

She's staring down at her plate. 'I wish I'd known,' she says quietly. 'I wish he'd said one word to me.' I hear the tears distorting her voice and how hard she's trying to keep them down. We have an unspoken rule between us, which started right after we came here. We don't cry around each other.

I try to picture Poppy contacting her. What could he have said? What would she have done then? It would have destroyed what little fragment of peace she ever found here. 'Do you?' I ask.

I watch her face. I wonder if she is picturing the same thing. 'Maybe not. Maybe it was the kindest thing to do.'

As we sit in silence I realize there was another thing too, and it makes me feel sad and old as I begin to understand it. My father was a handsome and powerful person. When we left him, he was a visionary and a leader. By the time he got here, he was old and wasted, sick and exiled. He wanted his wife and his daughter to remember him the way he was.

As I think back to his face the day I saw him in the library, I can see how little he wanted me to know he was my Poppy, to have his new identity supplant his old one. He was ashamed.

Just before eleven that morning I get a call at home from a woman at the Holy Cross Medical Center in Teaneck.

'Is this Prenna James?' she asks.

'Yes.'

'I have a package for you.'

'Really?'

'Yes. Do you want to pick it up? Or do you want to give me your home address and I will send it to you?'

'Do you know who it's from?'

'Andrew Baltos left it for you.'

'He did? Did he go somewhere? Did he get discharged already?'

'Oh.' She's silent for a couple of seconds. 'You don't know. I thought you knew.'

'What?' My pulse is pounding.

'I'm sorry to inform you Mr. Baltos is no longer with

us. He hanged himself in his hospital room at six o'clock this morning.'

I call Ethan from the car as I drive to Teaneck to pick up the package. I tell him what happened. I cry when I tell him and I don't even know why. Andrew Baltos was a murderer who single-handedly destroyed our future. He is very possibly the man who murdered my father, and it's better that he's gone.

These are tears of relief if anything, but as I picture Baltos in the hospital bed, longing to go home to his first girl, it all feels more complicated than that. His death seems to blend with the other deaths I've seen these last few days. I cry different kinds of tears for each of them.

The package is waiting with a receptionist at the front desk. It's my envelope, as I guessed it would be. Baltos wanted to return my stuff. I wait until I am home and in the privacy of my room before I open it to check that it's all there.

It is, and there's something more too.

Dear Prenna,

Theresa Hunt is dead. Her son, my son, Jason, is also dead. Allan Cotes is dead. I made some calls after you left, and that's what I found out. Josie Lopez is not dead, but her mother tells me she's been ill. I suspect it's only a matter of time.

I don't have any illness that I know of. If I had known, I never would have . . . It doesn't matter. I am the cause. I read your report. I know what's coming.

The two other people I've slept with since I've been here are Dana Guest and Robin Jackson. I've written their phone numbers and addresses below, along with Josie's.

Will you please help stop what I have done? I don't know what you can do, but I beg you to try.

I stare at it for a while. And then I fold it in half and retrieve the red folder that my father began. I go downstairs to the kitchen and hand them both to my mother.

I tried to be cool in my meeting with my mother and Mr. Robert yesterday, but by four o'clock that afternoon, I am sweating. I am pacing the floor of my room, glancing out the window to the street in front every couple of seconds.

At four-thirty I can't stand it anymore, and I go downstairs and out the front door and start pacing across the front lawn. At least that way I'll see her sooner if she comes.

My mother has been closed up in her room since I gave her the red file and the letter from Baltos. A few times I've overheard her speaking on the phone. I want her company, but I don't want to disturb her.

I stare at the street in front of our house, and I wonder how my mom wants this to go.

No, I know how.

I know because of the breakfast she made. I know because of the thing she said about the world waking up.

She wants Katherine to come. She wants to fix the damage that's been caused. She wants us to be okay. And for the first time, I think she wants more than that too.

I know in my heart that if Katherine comes, our lives are going to be better. It won't be easy, but we'll muddle through. My mother might even be happy for a few seconds. Would that be something? Hard to imagine, but not impossible.

At five I am resigned to my sorry fate, and at 5:02 a silver car pulls up and Katherine gets out of it. The driver is a grimlooking Ms. Cynthia, and I don't care. I run to Katherine and throw my arms around her. She looks shell-shocked but also happy to see me.

'Are you okay?' I ask her.

'I'm fine,' she says under her breath. 'But what did you *do*? I just had the weirdest car ride of my life.'

I practically crush her in my arms. I am so happy to see her, I am crying. 'Things are changing,' I say. I don't care who hears me. 'I have so much to tell you.'

After a few minutes Katherine gets back in the car to go home to her dad, but Ms. Cynthia lingers for another moment, glaring at me through the open window.

'You're not going to get what you want, you know.' She's a spider. She's full of poison.

I turn to her. 'What are you talking about?'

'You can flout everything we stand for, Prenna, everything we've tried to do.' She is practically spitting her words at me. 'But if you care about this young man of yours and you care about fixing the future, as you say you do, you can't have him. Not the way you want.'

'You're wrong.'

'You'll see.'

I can't hide my astonishment and my disgust.

'Try not to look stupid, Prenna.'

TWENTY-FIVE

Later that night I can't fall asleep.

I pack my bag for Friday night. What do you pack for a night like this? I gaze at the pile of dull cotton underwear in my drawer, the tank tops and boxer shorts I wear for pajamas. What can I do? Before now I never got to dream there would be a night like this. I throw in a box of Tic Tacs with a few peppermint ones shaking around the bottom. I add the little speakers for my phone.

I suddenly have an idea. I pull my desk chair into my closet so I can reach the highest shelf. I feel around for the New York Giants sweatshirt. I pull it down and shake it out. I hold it to my face and try to smell if there are any molecules of Ethan left in it.

I spend a few minutes making a playlist on my phone. Who knows?

I smile as a text pops up in the middle of it.

43 hours.

I glance at the time on the phone. I count in my head.
42 hours 40 minutes, I type.

A minute passes. *42 hours 39 minutes.*

I love you.

I love you.

I am surprised to hear a knock at my bedroom door
and my mother come in.

'You asleep?' she asks.

'No.'

'Can I talk to you for a few minutes?'

'Sure.' To my amazement she sits down on my bed.
The light is dim, just moonlight rolling in through my
window, but I see she's taken off her glasses again. She
has the red folder in her hands.

'I read through what you gave me.'

'Pretty incredible, huh?'

'Certainly is. And you said he killed himself?'

'Yes. Early this morning.'

She lets out a deep breath. She shakes her head.

'Reading his letter, I guess I can see why he did it.'

'I guess I can too.' She looks down at the folder. 'You
know you've given us something truly extraordinary
here. Between these names and our knowledge of the

future, we have a real chance to contain this illness. It's not something I ever dreamed could happen.'

Her face is as animated as I've ever seen it. I feel awash in pleasure and pride. 'You think so?'

'Unless there's some complexity we don't know about. Some other time traveler or . . .' She glances at me. 'Something else.' She takes my hand. 'But this information together with everything I studied as a physician and experienced in Postremo is fitting together in a way that makes me very, very hopeful.'

I've never heard her say that word. I have never seen these expressions on her face before.

'So Baltos brought the plague back with him to our time and started spreading it?'

'Not exactly. I suspect there was no plague where he came from, or at least not this plague. I suspect not that he brought it back, but that he started it. He harbored some virus or set of viruses, very likely originating from birds or pigs from his time. That's how it usually works. They were harmless to him and probably to other people in his time, but once the transmission was made, they were devastating to his lovers and close contacts here. It makes sense that the blood plague could begin in this way.'

'Okay,' I say slowly.

'This virus appears to be blood borne at this stage, but there's no clear information yet on how difficult or easy it is to transmit. There's no diagnostic test for it, but I hope with this information you've given me we'll be able to create one.'

I am starting to get an uneasy feeling about the ramifications of this. 'So when the leaders said we could cause harm to the natives by the microbes we carry, they weren't just trying to scare us?'

'They may have wanted to scare us, but it also happens to be true.'

'Not in the category of the pills?'

My mother looks distressed. 'No, different.' She sighs. 'I know how you're feeling about Mr. Robert and the rest. I feel the same way. I don't agree with their methods, but the rules are meaningful, for the most part. The discipline and caution they demand from us are crucial. Andrew Baltos was ruthless and sloppy. Taking a young woman's life, sleeping with multiple time natives, fathering a child. These are things we are respectful enough never to do.'

I nod. I know what she's saying is true. 'Do you think Mr. Robert and the leaders are going to leave us alone? I know they brought Katherine back, but it's hard to imagine.'

'If you stick to your terms, they will stick to theirs. If they break theirs, you will have the support of every member of the community I can muster.'

I hardly know who this person is. 'Really?'

'More than that, I'm hoping for a change in leadership. I'm tired of standing by. We had a meeting last night, and I've called another for tomorrow night including every member of my generation. I've spread the word about the pills already. I've shared it with the medical team, and it was a surprise to all but one. If I can run the meeting properly tomorrow, we're going to vote on a new slate of leaders, new counselors and a new set of policies. Or at least we'll start on it. I'm going to personally argue for getting rid of the surveillance altogether.'

I am stunned by this. Stunned by her tone and her conviction. I don't know who she is, but I am glad she's here.

She looks at me carefully. I see sympathy in her face, and I'm not quite sure what it's for. 'But not everything will change, you know.'

'The important stuff,' I say. I'm a little giddy. 'Getting rid of the leaders and the counselors? No more answering to Mr. Robert? Or that witch Cynthia? Getting rid of the glasses? That's more than I ever hoped for.' I can't wait to tell Ethan. He will be floored.

She takes my hand again. 'That's not really the important stuff.'

I don't love a certain sound I hear buried in the bottom of her voice. 'It's important to me,' I say childishly.

'If we want to set the world spinning back on its proper axis, put time back in her proper order, reverse the misdeeds committed by Andrew Baltos, we have to be more careful than ever. That's the lesson of Andrew Baltos, and it confirms much of what we feared. We aren't free here to live the way we want. We can't let the rest of the world know where we came from or how we came. It would be hopelessly disruptive and make it almost impossible to prevent time travel in the future. We have to keep our secret, and it's a burden for all of us.'

'It's hard, I know, but we can do that,' I say. 'As long as we can talk honestly with each other, it will be much less of a burden.'

Her face is eager. 'I agree with you about that. I agree we must be allowed to support each other.'

'So what else is important?'

She pauses. 'It's our first job to contain the changes that have been made. You and Ethan are heroes in that effort. But it's our second job not to make any more changes.'

'Okay.'

'And that means we have to be careful and disciplined all the time. We can't live like regular people. We can't choose our relationships like regular people. We can't start families like regular people. We can't risk starting new pandemics just as we're trying to bring this one under control. We have to be the solution, not the problem.'

'I understand that.' I feel tears coming to my eyes.

'We have to agree, all of us, not to form relationships or allow marriages outside the community.'

'You're talking about Ethan, aren't you?'

'I'm talking about all of us. I know it doesn't seem fair to you. And it's not. Ethan's done so much to help us.'

'He has. It isn't fair.'

'But what about the dangers to him? What about the possible seeds of a new plague? You've uncovered the birth of Dama Virus X right in front of us. You've seen both the beginning and the end. You understand it's not just the two of you at risk.'

We look at each other and I know the people we're both thinking about.

'Prenna, if you love him, think about what you can offer and what he'd be giving up. Beyond the question of illness, what about his chance to live an unrestricted life? To have a family?'

I put my hands over my face.

'I don't care what Mr. Robert or Mrs. Crew think. I have no respect or loyalty to them. But what would we tell the other members of our community if they saw you had found happiness with a time native?'

I try to stop the tears with my hands. She puts her arms around me, and I can feel we've both broken our rule now.

'We are all lonely, Prenna. We are all wishing for freedom. We all want to belong to this time – not just to skim over it.

We all desperately miss what we lost. Imagine the difficulty if every one of us tried to find your happiness?'

Time passes and I lean in to her. I give my whole weight up to her. She holds me like she hasn't since I was a baby. Since maybe ever. I feel like a baby, and I just want to rest. I feel like her baby.

'I am sorry, my darling,' she whispers to me.

◆ TWENTY-SIX

I don't bring the boring tank tops or the boxer shorts or the Tic Tacs. I've still got the playlist on my phone, but I know I won't play it. I hold the New York Giants sweatshirt for a long time before I put it back on the top shelf of my closet.

We meet at the parking lot of a trailhead at Haverstraw. Ethan comes toward me with his tent folded up under one arm and his one sleeping bag under the other. I think my heart will break.

As soon as he sees my face he knows something isn't right. His intuitive eyes are on mine, discovering the truth as always, but he keeps his voice light.

'Is it not Friday?'

'It is Friday.' I can barely keep my head up.

'Is this not our night?'

I feel my chin quivering. I wish it would stop. 'I think maybe it's not our night.'

He puts his things down on the bench at the trailhead. We start walking into the woods. He reaches for my hand. 'What happened?'

'Good things. That's what's so strange.'

'Tell me.'

It's easier, in a way, to be walking and not looking directly at his face. 'There was a second big meeting of the community last night. My mom organized it. They voted in new leaders. They fired the counselors in one shot and invited all community members who are interested in those jobs to submit applications. They voted out the pills and the glasses. They got rid of the systems of punishment and the so-called safe houses. They determined that the new counselors should actually provide support and encourage us to talk, not just browbeat and intimidate us.'

He glances at my face as we walk. 'Prenna, that is wonderful. I'm happy for you. For all of you.' He says it sincerely, but he's steeling himself for the next thing. 'Is your mother one of the leaders?'

'No. They wanted her to be, but she prefers to head up the medical team and focus all her energy on containing the virus Baltos started. She thinks they can stop it before it turns into the plague.'

'Who are they, then? The leaders?'

'Mostly people who were aligned with my dad at the beginning. People like my mother who've been marginalized and silenced since we got here. You only know one of them.'

'Who?'

'Me.'

'You are kidding.'

'No. I wasn't at the meeting when it happened. I found out about it from my mother when she got home. She said she didn't put my name up for consideration, but a couple hundred other people did.'

'Unbelievable.'

'I know.'

'That's my girl, Henny. You beat 'em and you joined 'em.'

I smile. 'I guess so. It's a heavy responsibility, though. I guess it's easier being a rebel than being in charge.'

Ethan nods. He looks sad. 'I have a feeling we're getting to my part of it.'

'Yeah.' I slow our pace.

'A rebel can have a native boyfriend, but a leader can't?' He's trying to sound sardonic, but he's not wrong.

We get to a rocky part by the river. I sit down and he

follows my lead. I have to look at him when I say this. 'It's not just that.' I hold his hands. 'I would give up all of that for you if I could. The problem is that the threat to you is real. Baltos proved it. He didn't bring back a preexisting plague. It was his contact with time natives that started it. My mom says we can hope to contain it, but not if we're sowing new seeds of it.'

Ethan puts his head down.

'What if everyone in the community was doing what we are doing? None of us knows how to avoid the risks because we don't understand what we're carrying yet or how it could spread.'

'Yet.' He lifts his head. He pounces on that word.

'Yet or if or never. There's no way to know.' I lean close. I need him to understand. 'Being with me would ruin your life, Ethan. It could ruin your health. It could destroy your hope of having any freedom, having a family. You can't give that up. I won't let you.'

'Being with you is all I want.'

I start to cry. How long could I hold it back?

He pulls me toward him and cradles me against his chest. 'From the first time I saw you right up the river from here, Penny, I never stopped thinking about you. I didn't see you again for two years and I thought about you every day. The fact that I was there when you came, that I can see the things I see, that we have taken this insane ride together. We are meant to be.'

I cry some more. I wipe my nose on my hand and look up at him. 'How can you say that? I'm not supposed to be here at all. It's wrong. Time doesn't want us to be together.'

'Time doesn't *want* anything. Isn't that what you said?'

'I did, but—'

'We *are* together. Maybe time is not the one in charge.'

I cry into his T-shirt. I get it wet. I love the feel of him and the smell of him. I love him. But my job is to protect him. I made sure he lived past May 17, and I'm going to make sure he keeps on living.

I love his living heart beating against my temple. For a long time it syncopates the sound of the river sliding by us.

'It's not over, Prenna. Someday you'll realize it too.'

I guess it's Monday evening when the knock comes at the door of my room. I think it's Monday. I'm not sure. I've spent most of the time since Friday night in my bed, and the hours and days kind of blend together.

It feels like a world-changing effort just to get out of bed and open the door. I don't really bother about the fact that I'm in pajamas and my hair is going in twenty directions and I haven't brushed my teeth in how long.

'Hi, Prenna.' It's Katherine. I can tell she wants to reach out and hug me, but she hasn't quite got the knack of physical contact yet.

'Hi, Katherine.' She's not wearing her glasses. She looks so young and pretty.

'Put on some clothes, okay?'

'Why?' I ask.

'Because we're going on a little trip.'

'Where?'

'You'll see. Come on.' She goes to my dresser and starts pulling things out of the drawers. She seems to understand it's not going to happen on its own.

I get back in my bed. 'I'm tired,' I say.

'That's what you said yesterday. And Saturday.' She hands me a pair of shorts, a T-shirt and a red bathing suit.

'Well, I'm still tired.'

'Just put them on.'

I sigh. 'Why the bathing suit?'

'Just put it on. You'll see.' She opens the door to my bathroom and points the way. In case I forgot. 'And brush your hair. And wash your face. And brush your teeth.'

I glare at her, but I'm too tired to be defiant.

Katherine's a lot more stubborn than she looks.

I carry the clothes into the bathroom. I put them on and get washed, trying not to look in the mirror as I do it. It's just depressing.

'Go get in the car,' she says. 'I'll be right there.'

'I thought I was supposed to be the leader.'

She laughs and marches me down the stairs. She stops off in the kitchen. I hear her talking to my mother, and she comes out carrying a picnic basket.

'Your mom packed us some treats,' she says brightly.

I peer in and see all my favorites, including mango smoothies and a new box of Mallomars. 'All this sympathy and I'm going to get super fat,' I mention dully as I follow her to her car.

Katherine plays music loud, all songs she knows I love, and we drive with the windows open. It does feel good to be moving.

'We can just talk, you know, Pren,' she says over the music and the wind. 'Thanks to you, we can talk about anything we want.'

I stare out the window. That's something I've hungered for since we got here. Now I don't know what to do with it. 'What should we talk about?'

Katherine has a look of mischief about her. She turns the music down. 'We could talk about how awful

Ms. Cynthia looks with her new haircut. How bad her breath is. How much fur Mr. Robert has creeping out of his nose.'

We try that for a while but it peters out. We both know they don't matter anymore.

Instead, we talk about the future. Not the far future, but the near one. I can tell she has something she wants to tell me. 'I was thinking I might apply to be a counselor,' she says. I can see she is shy about it.

'Oh, Katherine. That's the best idea.' I feel a stirring in my chest. I can't help it. What a beautiful thought. The worst of our community replaced by the loveliest.

We drive for a long time, and I can feel it when we're getting close to the ocean. I can feel the warm salty air in my face.

She parks near the lighthouse at Fire Island. We shed our clothes, pull socks off our tender feet, and skitter over the sand like newly hatched turtles. We hold hands and wade into the calm night ocean.

I look up at the glorious pink moon gazing at herself in the dark water. It makes my heart stir again. It's not a moon to take aim at; it's a generous moon with light enough to bathe in.

No matter how our hearts break, we bend toward life, don't we? We bend toward hope.

I think back to yesterday, late in the day when I heard a car pull up to the house, and even under two layers of blankets, I knew it was Ethan's car. I made my tentative way toward the window and watched him walk up to the front door with an envelope in his hand and drop it in the mail slot.

Halfway back to his car he looked over his shoulder and saw me standing in the window. He turned and lifted his hand to me. I pressed five fingertips against the glass. We both stood there, him a cutout against the pink sunset sky. I tried to hold back the crying until he was gone.

In the envelope I saw the newspapers and the cash we'd brought on our trip. I was going to leave it untouched in the top of my closet and shut the door, but my eye caught a bright yellow Post-it note stuck to one of the newspapers. I took it out and followed the arrow Ethan must have drawn to an article on the front page of the last paper, dated June 2021.

The article described in ominous terms the triumph of a billionaire oil and gas tycoon in his crusade to bring down the last of the regulations against carbon emissions, the last gasp of government hope to fight climate change. I didn't recognize the name, but I certainly recognized the face in the picture.

Whatever the name, Ethan knew and I know it is Andrew Baltos.

We didn't need proof to know we'd opened up the future. But it sure doesn't hurt.

When I fell asleep later, I dreamed of my brother Julius. He wasn't in the old world where I'd always dreamed him before. He was here, healthy and strong, striding up the front walk of a house a lot like our house, holding a bunch of yellow daffodils in his hand.

I think of that dream now as Katherine and I turn our faces up to a blanket of stars so vast and ancient and magnificent that you just know you are living in a world that has thought of everything.

Still holding hands, we swim out far beyond where our feet can touch. It's scary and uncertain, but it is also thrilling.

Because who knows what happens next?